LORD KIDRODSTOCK

I0682454

Stays

and

Gloves

Figure-Training and Deportment by Means
of the Discipline of Tight Corsets, Narrow High-Heeled Boots,
Clinging Kid Gloves, Combinations, etc., etc.

LONDON and PARIS

—

MCMIX

—

BIRCHGROVE PRESS
MMXI

Copyright © Birchgrove Press
All rights reserved.

http://www.birchgrovepress.com

ISBN:
978-0-9871953-0-2

Stays and Gloves was first published in 1909 by Roberts et Dardaillon in Paris. It was printed on hand-made paper in a limited edition of 330 copies with ten copperplate engravings by Del Giglio. The author is not known. *Stays and Gloves* was reprinted c. 1926 (with the original imprint date MCMIX on the title page) by the Librairie Artistique, 66, Boulevard Magenta, Paris, in a limited edition of 330 copies with ten copperplate engravings by G. Smit. This Birchgrove Press edition is based on the c. 1926 reprint. The text has been revised to enhance legibility: like many clandestine publications, the original edition is riddled with typographical errors.

Stays and Gloves

CHAPTER I

I had just reached the age of ten when my father died. At this period we lived in a nice-looking house. But the quarter bears that stamp of poverty which is all-prevailing in the East-End of London. The dwelling is in Shepherdess Walk, close to the City Road.

I went regularly to the district-school and was reputed a bad scholar. The master was kind, although we found his haughty manner very trying. He was content to go through his lessons. If he asked a question or made an observation, he did so briefly, in a manner devoid alike of politeness and roughness. Never did I see him in a temper. He rarely rebuked and struck more rarely still. On these latter occasions, it was a rap with the ruler upon the fingers as he passed. And he did not pause either to console or to reprimand the weeping child whom he had hit.

The death of my father brought about great changes. Without being rich, we had been comfortably off. My mother was always ill at ease in this quarter of poor people, she with her prettiness, refinement and distinction. She was also still young, for she was not quite eighteen years old when she brought me into the world.

After my father's funeral, my first recollection is the visit of a gentleman who was on very familiar terms with my mother and me although I had never seen him previously. After my father's death he was a daily caller. Sometimes he took my mother on his knees and kissed and caressed her. At these moments the faces of both were very red. At times she would seize hold of his arm and with a movement of her eyes make signs towards me. But the gentleman would laugh and reply:

"Absolute nonsense! What does that young innocent know of the fires of love?"

I disliked him and yet I was always glad of his visits, for he always brought me a toy or some sweets and sometimes both. Indeed he was not above playing with me. But — though whether inadvertently or purposely I do not know — he made me feel quite queer: for his manner of touching me as he raised me from the ground or as he rolled me over and over made feel ashamed and unnerved.

I no longer went to school.

The three of us would step into a very beautiful carriage drawn by two horses, and in Mr. Joe Baker's (for such was his name) fine turn-out, we would drive to the West-End, to Portland Place, to a beautiful mansion belonging to him and containing a vast number of grooms and maid-servants.

All the latter were pretty. They were both fair and dark, gentle and proud, but all were remarkable. They were not dressed as English domestics usually are, except that they wore, as is customary, the little linen cap, so stylish, light and charming. The other parts of their costume were of a picturesque nature. All wore aprons of brilliant coloured silk and a dress with no sleeves. On their hands and arms were exceedingly tight gloves of glazed kid, coloured black or dark brown, and very long, reaching above the elbow. I was struck by this particular feature in their costume. It seemed strange that humble maid-servants should wear such valuable gloves. My little brain, much puzzled, sought a solution of this mystery, but with no success. The events which I shall relate threw light upon the matter for me as they will not fail to do for the reader. For the time being, I could not get beyond this simple conclusion: that Mr. Joe Baker must posses a vast fortune if he could clothe his servants so sumptuously.

As I have said, we used to leave our house in Shepherdess Walk in the carriage and Mr. Baker would come himself to fetch us, but at times it was merely the carriage which would drive up to our door. We would lunch and dine with Mr. Baker who would not fail to remark at table that I was exceedingly ill-mannered, yet without giving the least suggestion as to how I should correct myself. His observation, always accompanied on his part with smiles and affability, did not fail to cover me with confusion. I sought to discover in what respect I was bad-mannered, but in vain and I finished by asking Mr. Baker what he found amiss in my behaviour. His sole reply was a fit of laughter, when my mother became greatly annoyed. She boxed both my ears and I remember that the pain was nothing to me as compared with my sense of the injustice of her act. I wept with grief and vexation, bursting into hysterical sobs, which exhibition had for result my being sent away to finish my luncheon in the servants' hall.

A maid came to lead me away and see after my meal. She was tall, dark, and stout with very big eyes looking blackly out from under heavy brows. Her lips were red and full, and the suspicion of a moustache was visible. Her thick arms carried without a single wrinkle the black, glazed kid gloves. She took me by the hand. I stamped and resisted, but in vain; she took me away without effort. I was, however, in a terrible passion due to my mother's injustice which I had never previously experienced. I let myself fall to the ground and tried to kick.

The maid took me in her arms. I struggled and cried, saying that I wanted to leave the house immediately. I tried to bite her. But we were already in the hall. Here she handled me as Mr. Baker had done, but with more insistence. The sensation due to the contact of the kid glove immediately calmed my anger. I became at once quite tractable, my mind being filled with a strong desire to obey this tall girl and do everything she wished. It was at this moment that she smiled at me pleasantly.

In the servants' hall, as she watched me eating, she frowned from under her heavy brows. Then in a rough voice, she ordered me to cease eating bread. To tell the truth, I was in the habit of eating a great deal of bread, far more than is eaten in England where they take scarcely any. I used at that time to stuff my mouth with bread between the courses and consequently had little appetite for meat and vegetables. My father had only laughed and used often to say that "in my gluttony for bread I was a true Frenchman." I repeated this saying of my father to the maid, whose name was Betsy.

She shrugged her shoulders disdainfully and replied that my father was a poor sort of man who had brought me up badly, or rather who had not brought me up at all, but all was going to change now.

My lassitude of a few minutes before was succeeded by a mood of excessive irritation. Her contempt for my poor dear father whom I so sincerely mourned, I found unbearable. I burst into bitter reproaches of Betsy's cruelty, assuring her that my father had been worth Mr. Baker a thousand times over. She roughly told me to hold my tongue, adding:

"You are an impertinent little boy!"

"No!" cried I. "It is you who are insolent. You have no right to speak of my father except with respect, as a servant should."

She turned pale at the insult and directed so terrible a look at me that I immediately regretted my imprudence.

Then appearing to recover herself, she rejoined:

"Not another word! Instead of gossiping, you would do well to eat this nice piece of underdone meat. It is better than stuffing yourself with bread."

So I tried to leave the bread alone, but so strong is habit that I began eating it again absent-mindedly, filling my mouth gluttonously.

"You disgust me!" said Betsy. "You perfect little gormandizer!"

The meal was however, at an end. She showed me fruits and jam and then replaced them in the cupboard without offering them to me. She said that as a punishment for my impertinence, I should be deprived of dessert. Then she came and sat close to me, putting one arm round my neck and patting my face in an affectionate way. I do not know if it came from her arm or from her glove, but the perfume which entered my nostrils intoxicated me.

"Your father ought to have whipped you," she said.

I made no answer. She continued: "Have you ever been whipped?"

"Never!"

"Well! You are going to be then! You deserve punishment."

"Really?" said I, escaping from her. "And who's going to whip me, I should like to know?"

"I am!"

She had already caught me in her powerful arms. I struggled, kicked, threatened, tried to bite and scratch her, without appearing to make the least effect upon her. This woman of thirty was very strong and had no difficulty in getting the better of a poor little child of my age. She gave me some sound cuffs on the ears which made me giddy. Then she put me down on the ground so violently that I almost had a fall. She gave me this order:

"Unbutton your clothes!"

"What?" said I, in astonishment.

"Take your knickerbockers down!"

I was about to obey her mechanically, when I was seized with a transport of anger and began stamping and shrieking. She then said:

"You refuse to obey me?"

"Why yes! I do refuse... You must be mad."

"Very well!" she replied. "You shall pay for this impertinence and for your rudeness at lunch at the same time."

In the twinkling of an eye, her quick fingers, in spite of her gloves, had unbuttoned my knickerbockers which she then proceeded to pull down to my heels. Pulling up my shirt, she laid me across her knees and gave me a very sound spanking which made me bellow and shriek. The slaps fell thick and loud while she cried to me:

"Shriek away, my young gentleman! Shriek as much as you like. No one will come to your aid. Presently I'm going to give you good reasons for crying yourself hoarse. That I promise you!"

After soundly spanking me, she set me on my feet again and told me to open the drawer of the sideboard, take the birch-rod which I should see there and bring it to her. Instead of obeying her, I rushed away, as she released me, nearly falling at full length on the floor on account of having my knickers down, and took refuge in the farthest corner of the room. With my face turned to the wall, I began to cry bitterly.

"One! Two!... Are you going to obey?"

I trembled at her voice and sobbing more than ever, as though my head was splitting, went to the sideboard. On finding the drawer, I was seized with a new fit of passion and crying worse than ever, took refuge once more in my corner.

She got up, seized the rod herself, and holding me by the ear, led me back to the chair. She then made me go down on my knees in front of her, and holding my head between her knees, she flogged me during long minutes, paying no heed whatever to my tears and entreaties.

"Another time I shall flog you till the blood comes, naughty little rascal! It's the only way to make you mend your ways."

I shrieked, rolling on the ground. She told me to get up. I did not want to listen to another word and lay where I was. Leaning down over me, she inflicted a caress on me, which far from calming me, unnerved me more than ever and made me fall into a state of dull stupefaction.

She dried my eyes, washed my face in cold water and led me back to the drawing-room, where ready to die of wretchedness and grief, I seated myself apart from my mother and Mr. Baker who at first paid no attention to me. It was only after some minutes that my mother glanced at me attentively, saying:

"Look at him! One would think he had been crying."

Mr. Baker, who was seated in a revolving arm-chair with his back towards me, slowly wheeled round. In his turn, he gazed at me, but in a contemptuous way which set my heart thumping. He laughed sarcastically, and then suggested:

"Let him alone. It only makes him conceited when attention is paid to him. I quite understand what it is. He's been impertinent and Betsy has punished him. She has a heavy hand — the wench!"

His face bore a strange expression as he said those words, and it seemed to me as though he were menacing me. My mother must have understood the words in the same way, for I saw her redden and lower her head in confusion. Rising to her feet, she looked at Mr. Baker apprehensively; so, at any rate, I interpreted her glance. Later, when the course of events had brought me light, I remembered that my childish intuition had not been at fault. My boyish mind did not easily reach this conclusion which I found very astonishing. I was so absorbed in my reflections on the matter that I trembled at hearing myself addressed in a stern voice by Mr. Baker.

"Well! your wits have gone wool-gathering? Listen to me and have done with your blue devil's stare! It is important that you should hear what I say to you. I have known your mother for a long time. She was my mistress during your father's lifetime."

My mother tried to interrupt him.

"Oh! Joe..." was all she could say.

As for me, without precisely understanding the meaning of the words, I saw that they contained something insulting to my father's memory and in my grief I burst into a storm of sobs.

My mother cried, too, and ran to me to take me in her arms, I avoided her and as she ran to me to take me in her arms, I put out my arms to push her away.

Mr. Baker again burst into a hard unpleasant laugh.

"Ha! Ha! He doesn't want you to come near him. Leave him alone, or I shall ask Betsy to take you into the Punishment Room. As for you, young man, this is what I have got to say to you. I have decided to marry your mother. The ceremony will take place next week. But I should be ashamed to show my friends a big boy so badly brought up as you. So you won't take part in the rejoicings. As your education has been horribly neglected and you cannot imitate your father's good manners because he hadn't got any, it is high time for me to think of crushing your stubborn will and teaching you how to behave in society. I have got money, and I am quite willing to spend a large sum in so praiseworthy an object. That is the reason why you will go to school to-morrow. You will be very comfortable there, for the establishment of Mrs. Flayskin is well managed. I may even say that it is a perfectly aristocratic boarding-school where you will meet with the heirs and heiresses to the greatest titles of the United Kingdom and to the biggest fortunes of America. If you behave yourself well and make progress, in a word, if the mistress declares herself satisfied with your conduct, you will pass your holidays with us. I don't think you are a bad child. You love your mother. That is good. Only, in your own interest, you must bend your unruly spirit. While there is yet time, you must uproot your instincts of revolt. You understand then? To-morrow you will leave the house. Betsy will take you. Come, give me your hand and let us be friends."

But already, like one distraught, shrieking in despair, my whole body convulsed with sobs, I had made a rush for the door wishing to flee this accursed house for ever. My idea was to gain the street and then go on foot to our own house to find once more the abode where my beloved father had died. Through the tears obscuring my sight I recognised Betsy. My childish fits were doubled in vain. They were powerless against those strong arms cased in black kid.

No sooner had I reached the outer door, than I felt myself caught in a vigorous grip.

CHAPTER II

Mrs. Flayskin, or, more correctly, Lady Flayskin, for by her marriage with Lord Flayskin she had entered the highest ranks of the English nobility — the class which has given the country its most illustrious soldiers and politicians — Lady Flayskin, then, was of American origin. Her beauty was of the American style which is often somewhat grotesque; that is to say, that while the general effect was pleasing, the details were defective. Her eyes were too deeply set and too far apart, one from the other. Her nose was too broad at the top and turned up at the tip like a bird's beak. Her appearance greatly impressed me, nevertheless. She was tall, she spoke softly and slowly, and could at will give a languid intonation to her words as befitted a blonde beauty.

When Betsy and I entered the room into which we were shown, we found Lady Flayskin, and with her a gentleman who appeared to me even more rigid and starched than Mr. Baker. By his nasal twang I took him to be an American. I was right. In New York he was a personage of note, for he was there actively engaged in the organisation of societies for the prevention of vice and assiduously busied himself with the private lives of other citizens.

He had also succeeded, thanks to his obstinate importunity, in getting the government to decide that it was the duty of magistrates to exercise astringent supervision over the morals of the people and by the severity of punishments inflicted, to check every deviation from the narrow path of purity calculated to set a bad example.

In his present surroundings, he seemed entirely at his ease and quite at home.

When we entered, he addressed Lady Flayskin. After fixing on me his round, cold light grey eyes he remarked:

"Another pupil for you?"

"Why, certainly."

"He appears to me to be in need of supervision."

"All have to be controlled and punished."

"I think so too!"

"Oh! you and I know that we have long held identical opinions."

"That does us credit. In truth, the world would be a better place than it is if everyone was imbued with the conviction that youth requires moral training."

"Which only the rod can impart."

"Very true."

This conversation to which I listened open-mouthed was not reassuring.

I had already tasted the whip as applied by the rough hand of Betsy and did not feel tempted to renew its acquaintance. My little posterior still smarted from the whipping of the day before.

After Betsy had explained who I was, and had hugged me in her big arms, covering my face the while with a rain of kisses in effusiveness which I found more astonishing than affecting, Lady Flayskin entrusted me to the keeping of an under-mistress who had just entered the room in hurried response to the summons of an electric hell.

The latter was a thick-set dumpy woman of incredible mobility. Even when she was not speaking and was sitting in her chair, all her body moved: eyes, nose, lips, and bust. She had movements for asking questions, for doubting, for hesitating and for signifying approval. Yet this was not through lacking a fine large tongue, as I was able to notice. During the few moments required to conduct me through the corridor to the class-room assigned to me, she found means to tell me a great many most curious things. Among other items of information, she told me that Lady Flayskin was a person of real distinction, a typical member of the aristocracy. That the profession of school-mistress was with her nothing less than a sacred call. That as I could easily see, she had no need whatever to undertake occupation of any kind. That thank God! — the late regretted Lord Flayskin had left his wife an immense fortune. Then she broke off suddenly and enquired if I wore stays?

I was much surprised at the question and although the

circumstances of my present position were by no means of a sort to incite me to gaiety, the idea that I could have stays on, made me burst into laughter.

Immediately this person who had been all smiles and pleasant chat, changed countenance with a suddenness which inspired me with terror. My laughter was choked in my throat. With nostrils distended, her eyes full of menace, the stout little woman shook my arm roughly, pulling and pushing me here and there as though I had been the handle of a pump and she had resolved to pump out of me my crowning irreverence.

"Little wretch! What possesses you to make you laugh like that? If you are not accustomed to stays those I am going to put on you will make you suffer. We shall then see if you are still in a laughing mood."

We had reached the class-room. We found no pupils therein. All were in the dormitory, it being the time when girls and boys had to wash their hands before appearing at table. But the mistress under whose orders I was to study was still there. She proved to be a narrow strip of a woman with straight tow-coloured hair, as angular and sparing of gesture as my fat, dark-haired and black-eyed conductress was rotund and vivacious.

"Mrs. Stuart," said the dumpy woman, bowing pleasantly to the thin one, "this is young Sanderson of whose coming you have already heard. Shall he sit down to table as he is, or do you wish him to be dressed like the others?"

"What a question!" replied the other with a shrug of her lean shoulders. "Certainly it is unfitting that he should be different from the others. It would be notorious disorder and nothing less. Has not Lady Flayskin given you any instructions on the matter?"

"She must have forgotten. I neglected to ask her for precise instructions."

"Then the duty devolves upon me. Go immediately to the store-room and get things to fit him. If luncheon is finished, he will have to eat by himself, that's all. But I am resolved that he shall not mingle in those outrageous clothes with the pupils. It would be a case of the wolf in the fold!"

I did not understand in the least what was required of me; but with feelings more affected than I can tell, I quietly followed my conductress who now took me to the outfitting establishment. Here a vast number of little girls' dresses were hung up by hooks, while boxes containing boots with high heels were arranged in their order of size upon the shelves. There were drawers containing glazed kid gloves. Others contained petticoats, dressing-jackets and pairs of stays. Then again there was a little girls' drawers department. In short, it was a typical wardrobe.

She began by taking my measurements with a great deal of vivacity. Her hands went hither and thither over my body and irritated my nerves. I became ill at ease and ashamed. She noticed my confusion and only laughed.

She quickly took my clothes off and found fault with the cleanness of my body, although Betsy had washed me all over that same morning. She therefore took me into an adjoining room which proved to contain a bath. I was plunged into the water and abundantly soaped. Her hands affected me indescribably. She seemed to put both malice and craft into her movements. When I appeared to her sufficiently white and clean, she dried me, delaying the operation longer than appeared necessary, and then led me back again to the clothes store.

She began by rigging me out in a little sleeveless chemise such as girls wear. Then she put on my legs very long stockings of black spun silk. After that, she decked me out in a little girl's drawers and a pair of stays which she tight-laced with all her strength, almost preventing me from breathing. The stiff whalebones then proved painful. But this physical discomfort was as nothing in comparison with the shame I felt at being thus dressed up in a fashion so little in accordance with my sex. Like all children of my age, I was not a little proud of being a boy. It seemed to me that this costume changed me undoubtedly into a girl.

I was not at the end of my martyrdom.

My shame increased and became intolerable when she attached the stockings to the stays by garters, and put elegant boots on my feet.

The latter were very narrow, arched, buttoned boots with an exaggerated instep, and very high Louis XV heels; "French" heels, as we say in England. They went very high up the calf of my legs and the material was kid. The toes were excessively pointed and highly varnished.

They would no doubt have appeared to me elegant and pretty enough if worn by some lady or young person of the gentle sex, although at that time I had not yet paid much attention to ladies' feet.

When I comprehended that they were going to replace my flat-heeled boots, my good, laced boots so serviceable for running and walking, they appeared to me grotesque, odd and ridiculous. It seemed to me that I had never yet set eyes on such boots. I was ready to laugh and cry at the same time. I stood there looking in a stupefied way at the boots in the hands of the under-mistress, the latter being on the point of putting them on my feet. She became annoyed at my listlessness.

"Well, what possesses you? When will you be done looking at me in that stupid way?"

"You are surely not going to put those boots on my feet?"

"Then you suppose wrong! I am going to put them on you at once."

"In the first place, I could never walk and run with those high heels!"

"You will get accustomed to them. By paying a little attention, you will succeed in walking very well with those heels. That will cure you of your naughty temper. Run? I absolutely forbid you to run. There is no running here!"

"I won't put on those boots! I won't let you put them on me! Nobody shall put them on me! No! No! No!"

"Now then! What ails you now? Put out the foot! Immediately!"

I was intimidated and obeyed mechanically. She put on the boot, and I had to press with all my weight on the ground, giving little kicks to make my foot enter, being horribly crushed and squeezed in the process.

With a button-hook, she immediately fastened up the boots and I experienced at the instep a horrible feeling of discomfort. The same operation was then gone through with the other foot. I stood up and immediately nearly fell down. She scolded me, laughing the while, then told me to take a few steps. This I did in a tottering way. My legs shook under me and with these heels I seemed to be walking on stilts slipping from under me. It was quite a new sensation.

The insecurity of my steps gave me an impression of great weakness and I was in a state of consternation.

I got as far as a large mirror, level with the ground along the wall opposite the door, between two cupboards. Mechanically I looked and was transfixed by what the mirror revealed. I saw with wretched surprise a face which was the reflection of my own. I saw its look of shame and its tear-dimmed eyes. Yes! I saw myself in a little girl's drawers with bare arms and shoulders, wearing ridiculous wretched stays; absurd stockings and hateful, uncomfortable boots, grotesquely arched and high.

At the sensation of the hand of the mistress upon my shoulder, I trembled. She was tying shoulder-straps to my corset, but the leather of this appliance for making me keep my chest well up was very thick and stiff. She pressed herself against me and put her cheek close to mine. I saw in the glass her amused, smiling expression; her large face contrasting with the despairing features against which it was held.

I should have long remained staring at this picture, for my power of volition seemed to have died within me, if she had not roughly burst in upon my thoughts.

"We've no time to lose. You must dress and eat a scrap of something in your fingers. You can see that playtime has already begun and soon the bell will ring for work to start again. It won't do for you not to be in your place on the very first day. It would be a bad example."

As she spoke, she pulled me away from the glass and her quick hands busied themselves in the task of dressing me. I let her do as she liked, lost in my thoughts. Playhours, she had told me, had begun; and I could not hear a sound save the clattering on stones of heels of the same pattern, doubtless, as those I was myself condemned to use.

What then could be the meaning of this play, which was conducted in silence?

How little it resembled the playground of that good parish

school I so sorely regretted! There the master stood apart from us, looking at us and seldom speaking. His few words were a remonstrance addressed to any scholar who was not sufficiently exerting himself, or who was altogether neglecting to play, and always in those calm even tones. He was indeed in the habit of telling us, as though he were citing a maxim, that exercise ought to be violent and work tranquil.

I was dressed. The mistress pushed me in front of the mirror. Except for my short hair, I looked a girl, indeed a pretty girl, if I may say so. This conclusion gave me little pleasure.

I was thoroughly sick at heart.

Still guided by the under-mistress, Mrs. Eagle, I reached the dining-hall, which had been vacated by everyone a quarter of an hour before. The cloth had already been removed from the immense table, but a napkin had been spread and a knife and fork placed thereon for me. I had to sit down and do honour to the food which a maid brought me. I was served by the mistress. I managed to eat, but at each mouthful, a lump seemed to rise in my throat and nearly choke me.

I had the habit not unusual with little boys, of leaning far forward over my plate and eating quickly. But this was now out of the question. The leather shoulder-straps cut into my flesh and the bones of my corset were very painful so soon as ever I attempted to lean forward. My unhappiness took away my appetite and I ate without pleasure and consequently not very quickly.

The under-mistress, however, pressed me to eat. She cut up my meat and scolded me.

At length the cheese was brought and I ate more rapidly and was again scolded. This time my offence consisted in having let a little butter fall on my white muslin bodice, whence it threatened to slip on to the sash of azure-hued silk with which I had been adorned.

We left the dining-hall and went into the school-room where the pupils were already taking their places. The vigour and energy of my under- mistress saved me for the nonce. By dint of hustling me along, she succeeded in getting me to enter the room with the last comers. Although the distance was so short, I had more than twenty times nearly measured my length on the floor thanks to my abominable heels. But she had roughly pushed me and half carried me along, appearing to attach vast importance to our not arriving after the others.

Her face was smiling, out of breath though she was, as she dragged me by the hand right up in front of the high desk where the scraggy Mrs. Stuart was enthroned. She replied by a nod of the head, as abrupt as though caused by pulling a trigger, to the profound curtsey with which she was honoured by graceful, dumpy Mrs. Eagle. The under-mistress shook my arm roughly, whispering:

"You too have got to salute!"

I did as I had been accustomed to do at the parish school when saluting our stiff and starched schoolmaster. That is to say, I executed a sort of military salute. I rapidly raised the forefinger of my right hand to the level of where I had been used to wearing a cap, and with equal celerity let my hand fall again to my side.

The stifled laughter which came from behind me did not have the effect of reassuring me. Mrs. Stuart, however, had risen to her feet as though worked by a spring, displaying in the action the flat charms of her lengthy body. With finger outstretched threateningly, she snapped out:

"The whole class shall receive punishment for this lack of politeness to a newcomer and to my friend Mrs. Eagle."

Silence reigned once more as though by the enchantment of fear. Mrs. Stuart then turned to me, meantime slowly jamming her glasses upon a nose as long and thin as the blade of a knife. She then fixed a prolonged stare upon me as though she had not so much as set eyes on me a short time previously when I was in boy's clothes.

When she had finished her contemplation which lasted two good minutes, and appeared to be going to last an eternity, she negligently let her pretentious folders fall and to my great consternation pronounced these words:

"I recognise the talent of Mrs. Eagle... No, dear friend, it is useless for you to protest! You have extraordinary skill. I said the same thing only yesterday to Lady Flayskin and Mr. Gostock... There you are, young man, so well fitted out that anyone would declare you were a little girl, though certainly a very badly-behaved one. A salutation is not made in that way. And your steps are too long. But your heels will teach you that without anyone's help. The curtsey, however, is another matter. You must learn that from us. What is your name?"

"Jim... Jimmy."

"James? Very good. In the future I shall call you Alice. It is right that you should have a woman's name as your dress is feminine."

At this fresh insult, I could not contain myself and burst into hysterical sobs.

This time, in spite of the threat of a moment before, laughter broke out behind me quite openly and distinctly. Mrs. Eagle laughed also. And although Mrs. Stuart made no sound, her long thin nose quivered, her thin lips twisted, her eyes became fixed in a horrible doll-like stare. This, as I afterwards discovered, was her manner of laughing, and very disagreeable it was.

As to myself, the shame I felt at being called by a girl's name was so overwhelming that I was unable to experience any additional shame for the moment. The laughter, the grimace of Mrs. Stuart, this and all the rest had no further effect upon me. I was, as it were, beyond all feeling.

"Will you have the kindness to take Miss Alice to her place?" said Mrs. Stuart. "There, to that unoccupied desk between Miss Carrie and Miss Lizzie."

I was taken to the indicated seat and left now to my own resources as to my manner of behaving. But my environment seemed pitted against me. As the lesson (it was geography) continued, I again became the butt of my fellow-pupils. "Butt" is a perfectly correct term in this connection. Not only was I the object of sly looks from all quarters, but I was also the target for balls of chewed paper well-soaked in saliva, and a storm of pellets rained around me. This attack provoked in me a healthy revulsion of feeling. My masculine instincts were roused and I wished in turn to attack my persecutors. For the moment I became oblivious of the girlish frippery dishonouring me.

The class-room was fairly capacious although adapted for only twenty pupils. Each had his separate desk, which did not touch that of his neighbour. In front of the teacher's desk, at the back of the room, near the wall, whence the mistress could at a glance command every thing, ran a kind of broad gangway separating the two rows of desks. On the boys' side, where my own place was, there were eight places occupied, counting mine. Four desks were vacant. On the girls' side all the twelve desks were occupied.

I looked about me openly, boldly facing the tempest of covert malice, a cyclone in which there was less of thunder than of hail and rain. Suddenly a ball of paper, more skilfully directed than the others, flattened itself against my lips. I had clearly seen who had propelled it. In a moment, I was on my feet and, raising with my two hands as high as I could the petticoats which impeded my progress, rushed towards the authoress of the insult. For it was a girl, though all, girls and boys alike, were in petticoats. I did not reflect that I ought to have been able to feel only contempt for my aggressor. I had, however, not reckoned with the horrid heels of my hateful boots. At the moment when I reached my foe, who, for her part, was so terrified that she made no attempt to escape and contented herself by manifesting her fear in heartrending shrieks, my heels slipped beneath me and I fell down headlong on the floor. I nevertheless had time to seize and cling fast to the girl whom I thus dragged with me from her seat in my fall. By a vigorous twist of my body, I got on top of her holding her down while dealing at the same time several sound blows with my fist upon her face. Meantime she shrieked "Help! Help! Murder!" with all her might.

The thin wiry arms of Mrs. Stuart came and rescued the little girl from my terrible grip.

The lean mistress, without a moment's hesitation, had rushed down the steps of her desk, covering at a gallop the few yards which separated her from the writhing mass on the floor, while the boys clapped their hands with delight at each blow I gave. The girls wept with fear.

Mrs. Stuart pinched and twisted my ears between her crooked fingers. I at once released my victim and rose to my feet. My enemy lay motionless on the ground, her legs stretched out. One would have imagined she was dead, had not her deep breathing and the rise and fall of her bosom proved her to still belong to the land of the living. The mistress, still holding my ear, led me back to my place, which I reached after several stumbles due to my heels and in a very crestfallen state of mind.

Mrs. Stuart stood before me as I sat at my desk. She haughtily surveyed me with her arms crossed upon her breast, then, touching me here and there she examined the damage done to my costume. The beautiful azure-blue silk sash was tumbled about out of recognition. With my right hand, I had split the fine, glazed, black kid glove which covered my arm up to the elbow and above it. And in my exceedingly short white muslin skirt was a rent. The mistress pointed out a rip here and a tear there in a hard, calm voice as through she were making an inventory.

Her tones were the same when she estimated the damage I had occasioned to the toilet of my enemy. I had indeed, in vigorously rolling the little girl on the ground, caused great disorder in her dress. One of her fine black gloves had been pulled inside out and the buttons dragged off, while the other, torn open, showed the palm of the hand.

Having finished her examination, the mistress went back to her high desk with great dignity. She announced that the lesson would stop for the time being, and that in consideration of the gravity of what had happened, she intended asking Lady Flayskin to come into the class-room to decide upon the punishment to be given after a rapid investigation had shown the relative guilt of each culprit.

In fact, she immediately despatched one of the pupils to the directress.

I did not know what was going to follow, and anyhow I little cared. I was filled with a sense of the justice of my cause and my combative instinct had not yet subsided. I only regretted that the time had not been long enough to enable me to give my enemy much more severe punishment. I said to myself, she should lose nothing through having to wait.

Nevertheless, the profound silence which reigned in the class-room ought to have given me matter for reflection. Everyone seemed overwhelmed. It looked as if something heavy weighed upon all these youngsters; as if, in fact, things were going to happen, for my fellow-pupils had had more experience than I.

To begin with, Lady Flayskin made a majestic entry. She was accompanied by Mr. Gostock, the austere American Puritan whose pale, cold eyes had already so strongly impressed me a short time before. As these august visitors entered, all the pupils rose in their places, I myself imitating the others. Mrs. Stuart left her desk and went respectfully to meet the head-mistress.

All this ceremonial began to make me uneasy. I felt a vague apprehension that it portended no good for me. I had a shrewd notion that the head-mistress, this haughty member of the aristocracy, was not a person who cared to be disturbed without reason.

I was right.

Mrs. Stuart began by explaining the incident in a sufficient impartial way. It was a question of laughter and balls of paper. She said that she was herself upon the point of intervening when I, in my unreasonable impatience, had taken justice into my own hands. So far she only spoke the truth. Matters took another turn when she added that I had perhaps been mistaken, for it was quite uncertain if Clara Weecock had been the culprit who had propelled the little missile, and that possibly she had paid for the offence of another. She added that Clara had, in any case, paid already, as I had rushed upon her with a storm of blows from my fists on her face. The conclusion to be established was that I was a perfect little savage who must be civilised as soon as possible or more serious results would follow.

It was in vain that I had tried to attract the kind attention of the head-mistress by adopting the usage I had learnt at the parish school. That is to say, in order to gain permission to speak, I had, with the object of correcting a mistake upon the part of the mistress, energetically rubbed my middle finger against my thumb; the finger then struck the palm and produced a loud clack. The directress turned round at this noise and looked at me. Hitherto she had not glanced in my direction. I made my signal with renewed energy, thinking I was about to obtain that permission to speak for which I was so impatient. She turned, however, to the mistress and said quietly:

"Make him stop, please."

There was no need to tell me to stop. I had immediately become quite still with, as it were, a heavy weight upon my heart, feeling crushed by the injustice of my treatment.

Lady Flayskin asked Mr. Gostock:

"What is your opinion?"

He replied without hesitation:

"They should both be whipped."

"That is also my opinion."

Little Clara began to cry out, declaring that she had done nothing. This lie kindled my anger anew. I declared that it was entirely her fault and that I had clearly seen her take aim and propel the disgusting pellet all saturated with saliva, making it strike me in the mouth.

The directress harshly told us to be quiet. She had removed her glazed, black kid glove and exhibited a large arm very plump and white. Its appearance of strength boded ill for the unfortunate little posteriors doomed to be whipped.

Mr. Gostock interrupted her:

"I beg you, my lady, don't take this trouble yourself." The lady smiled graciously:

"Ah! I read your mind! You wish your protégée, Miss Sinclair, to administer the punishment."

"I beg you to allow her."

"The permission is granted. Miss Sinclair, have the kindness to apply the birch with all the energy of which you are capable. Begin with Miss Clara, so that this lout Alice may see what awaits her."

Miss Sinclair immediately stepped forward. She was a really pretty girl of from fifteen to sixteen years of age, very slender, but with firm, rounded arms which gave redoubtable promise of that rigorous action to which Lady Flayskin had appealed.

At this moment I saw the American's dull eyes light up. There passed over them a flame, as it were, a blaze which immediately died away again. A little colour came to his cheeks, also disappearing immediately. Doubtless he experienced pleasure in seeing this pretty girl whip naked posteriors, but he did not think it fitting to display his feelings.

Miss Sinclair had already seized hold of Clara who shrieked to her to spare her, while again declaring her innocence.

As for me, I bit my lips till they almost bled, and clenched my fists, promising myself that I would strangle hateful Miss Sinclair if she should dare to lay a hand on me. But those ridiculous gloves in which they had rigged me out, prevented me from doubling my fists as I should have liked and I felt myself insecure upon those hateful heels which made me sway even when I was not walking.

Miss Sinclair had laid a hand on Clara's shoulder who walked sobbing to receive her punishment.

She was told to lean over the big table at the foot of the high desk where the mistress sat enthroned. To speak more correctly, she had to lie upon the table face downwards and forwards. With a dexterity, an ease of movement, an absence of gesture which spoke of habit, Miss Sinclair raised the petticoats of Miss Clara, whilst the victim's hands were immediately imprisoned in the long lean claws of the long Mrs. Stuart. After Miss Sinclair had adroitly pinned the skirts to the shoulders of the little martyr, the young girl unbuttoned the drawers, which she lowered to the heels.

The drawers were very curious. They consisted of a very tight garment which revealed to view the exact shape of the parts covered. I had never seen a similar garment. It was in fact, a pair of drawers made of black glazed kid of exactly the same material and shade as the long gloves we were obliged to wear. The hinder parts of Miss Clara were fully exposed, white and rounded. It was, upon my word, a very pretty pair of hemispheres and although hitherto I had never thought of attaching any importance to what little girls sit upon, I could not help being moved by the sight, though I had no idea of analysing the reasons of this curious emotion, which stirred me more deeply than I can well say. As to fear, I felt none whatever. The immediate future, however, was to prove for me terrible enough.

Miss Sinclair slowly drew off her long gloves and with a collected air hung them over the rail of the high desk. She was doing her task without forgetting the smallest detail, and immediately had her reward in a smile from correct Mr. Gostock; a smile, indeed, which was really a horrible grimace, or appeared to me such.

The directress then addressed Clara:

"Well, Miss! I hope you feel ashamed to be exhibiting the nudity of the lower part of your back to the gaze of the whole class? Are you sorry for your naughty folly?"

"Pardon me, my lady, I beg you."

"Are you going again to propel balls of paper soaked with your spittle?"

"My lady!... I declare to you... I threw none. The little boy made a mistake."

"Do you see?" said the directress to Miss Sinclair. "She is incorrigible. Punish her well therefore, as much for her lie as for her fault. Don't spare her."

Clara moaned and wept in a stifled way, as her petticoats covering her head hardly let her breathe. A spasmodic quiver ran up her little thighs, trembling already in anticipation.

Miss Sinclair did not appear to be at all in a hurry to begin the work of execution. Yet certain signs of animation in her manner sufficiently revealed her pleasure. Her fine dark eyes sparkled. Her pretty half-opened mouth showed her dainty, even, white teeth. She passed her pointed rosy little tongue over her crimson lips like a gourmand with his favourite dish before him. She had also lifted her head in saucy pride and I remember that her fair hair seemed like a mass of burnished gold.

She proceeded with a quiet step and with quite the dignity of a queen to a cupboard against the wall between two large maps. Miss Sinclair was not troubled by her high heels. One would have thought she wore no boots at all, so easy were her movements. Her step was as noiseless as it was rhythmic.

She opened a drawer of the large cupboard and cast an inquiring glance within. After a pause, she took therefrom a birch which she balanced in her hand. Then with a look of contempt and a shrug of the shoulders she threw it back again. Her hand searched anew, and this time produced a very terrible implement as it appeared to me. It was a thick long rod, terminating in a steel-like point.

All these deliberate movements and preparations inspired a perfect paroxysm of terror in her who was about to be whipped. That was clear to every eye in the class by the writhings of the nude globes. They jutted out behind as though to meet the birch there was no escaping, and then contracted, as though to avoid it, all the while wriggling as though already stung a thousand cutting blows and moving from side to side as if the cruel pain were already more than they could bear. In short, they spoke with a dumb eloquence which was nothing less than poignant. And, in point of fact, both boys and girls showed their feelings by their bated breath. Without possibility of doubt, there was none more affected than I myself, not even perhaps excepting the poor little girl who waited for the first blow to fall. And while waiting — for I knew that soon my turn would come — I felt my fine courage of a few moments before melting into air, and my own anguish, became more and more intense. I knew that there would not even be any necessity to hold my hands. I was already at the mercy of beautiful Miss Stella Sinclair, whose calmness was, so to speak, a miraculous chain which bound me. I was spellbound. Had a miracle taken place before my eyes, I should have been unaffected by comparison. With that rod brandished in warlike fashion in her hand, this fair young girl appeared to me an image of terror, an evil divinity. She was in truth a young she-devil in spite of her ravishing beauty. It was my fate to assure myself of the fact, by the eyes to begin with, in my skin afterwards.

She placed herself behind her victim and asked in exquisitely sweet, silvery tones:

"Are you ready?"

"Yes! Yes!" came the reply in broken accents, as though wrung from a mind in mortal terror.

If Clara was ready, Stella was not, and I perceived that her question was designed simply to warn the child that the moment of punishment was at hand. Machiavelli-like, Stella desired to sharpen anew the heartrending anguish of her victim. The shaking and quivering of the bare stern showed that the object of astute Stella had been attained.

She stepped forward, stepped back again, extended her arm flourishing the rod, then again stepped forward. Evidently she was calculating her distance. But she gave much more time to her calculations than was necessary. That was certainly the opinion of her victim, for she cried out:

"Do for the love of God begin! It ought to be finished by now!"

This ingenuous complaint spoilt Stella's effect. Her careful acting broke down. In harsh tones, she replied:

"It is not for you to give me orders, Miss. The signal for beginning will not be given by you. I am charged with the task of whipping you and naturally I wish to do my duty conscientiously. What have you to reply to that?"

"Nothing! Nothing!" sobbed the victim. "But I beg you, I entreat you, don't delay any more. Get it done as quickly as possible. Oh, how I wish it were already finished!"

"That I can well understand," replied crafty Stella, in her witch-like tones. "You shall be well whipped I promise you, so your desire is natural, I feel myself in good form to-day. My energy is unusual. I feel a sensation of nervous force and I thank our dear directress, gracious Lady Flayskin, for having kindly entrusted me with the task of punishing you. I am not about to prove unworthy of her confidence, as I beg to declare."

"Oh! Oh!" cried Clara.

"This begins to be intolerable," said Miss Sinclair. "Yes or no, are you going to hold your tongue? And will you be so kind as not to agitate your impertinent hindquarters in so indecent a fashion. Keep still, or I will strip off the skin and make the blood run in streams down to your heels."

"Pardon me! Have pity on me!" moaned the wretched child.

But her prayer finished in a loud shriek. The punishment had begun.

How that diabolical rod whistled and bent when wielded by the supple and vigorous though childlike arm of the flogger! Never should I have imagined that this bit of a girl had so much strength. My imagination no doubt increased the terror of the spectacle. If only I had been dressed in my knickerbockers, with strong laced boots on my feet, instead of wearing those unsteady high-heeled boots and girl's skirts, I should have known how to face Miss Sinclair. I would have soundly boxed her ears and shown her how a self-respecting boy treats a girl who intentionally annoys him. But rigged out as I was, and sorely tried by the multiple experiences of the past forty-eight hours, it is not surprising that I had little courage left. It is known, too, how the mind reacts upon the body. I felt extremely weak and my body still smarted from the whipping which Betsy had given me the day before. Curious to relate, too, as I looked at Miss Sinclair operating upon the bare flesh of unfortunate Clara, my mind called up the vision of the powerful maidservant. The white arm of the young girl became transformed. It was the thick arm of Betsy that I saw, the thick resolute arm gloved in glazed black kid upon which my clenched hand had used itself in vain. So realistic was the vision that I forgot the presence of Clara. It was me receiving the blows, crying and begging for mercy.

Alas! what was then but a horrid nightmare was about to become a grim reality.

I listened as in a dream to the dreadful whistling of the rod wielded by the untiring graceful arm of pretty Miss Sinclair. I heard the sobs, cries and entreaties of the victim, and her promises of amended conduct in the future. She confessed to having flipped the ball of paper and she accused her neighbour of having instigated her to commit the heinous deed. Then she said that she did not wish to accuse anyone. She had acted upon her own initiative alone. She shrieked in a heartrending manner, imploring for pardon and pity, declaring that she could not endure any more suffering, that she was going to die, that the whip had never hurt so much before.

She promised not to recommence her offences and implored Lady Flayskin to intervene and stop the flogging. Then she entreated Mr. Gostock to intercede with the directress that the latter might take pity upon her and pardon her.

She could not have entreated a deafer ear. For though at the time I was too much affected to notice Mr. Gostock, my observations later on showed me that this gentleman experienced the height of pleasure in watching the whipping of boys and girls by charming little Miss Sinclair. For from being likely to intercede for the termination of the punishment, his prayers would, on the contrary, have been for a continuation of operations, so enamoured was he or this kind of spectacle. This curious disposition of mind on the part of the gentleman will be clearly shown by the events which followed and which I shall relate in their own place. I must not anticipate.

No answer was made to the entreaties of the victim. Lady Flayskin, always the flawless and faultless woman of fashion, never for a moment forgetting that she was a rich American and a member of the innermost circle of British aristocracy, assumed a variety of attitudes while talking to Mr. Gostock, who replied to her in equally lofty tones. But, never for a moment did he cease to watch the elegant motion of the graceful white arm wielding the rod with unfailing energy and skill, and as gracefully as though it had been a fan.

At length, after a furious blow, to which reply was given in a despairing shriek, the torture ended.

Wretched Clara, slipping down upon her knees, wept with her head in her hands at the side of the table upon which she had been whipped. No one paid any further attention to her. Miss Sinclair, on the other hand, received many congratulations.

The directress inquired in tones of some anxiety:

"I trust you are not over-fatigued?"

"Not in the least, dear Lady Flayskin."

"What energy! What skill!" exclaimed Mr. Gostock. "Allow me to congratulate you very sincerely, my dear, charming Miss Sinclair. But truly... You are not fatigued? No? I am afraid you do not feel equal to conducting the second whipping."

"It is now the matter of a boy's... ahem! You understand my meaning? If the rod is not applied with severity, it will only cause him to laugh."

"Make your mind easy on that score, dear Lady Flayskin. I will make him shriek!"

At this assurance, of such interest for myself, the enthusiasm of Mr. Gostock knew no bounds. In tones thrilling with joy and admiration, he suggested:

"Rest yourself, if only for a moment, dear Miss Sinclair and take some refreshment."

"I am much obliged to you," replied Miss Sinclair, in her most bewitching tones.

In response to the electric bell, a maid came and was given an order. She returned a moment afterwards with a decanter, three wine-glasses and some biscuits. Miss Sinclair was the first to be handed a glass of old port, needless to say with much effusion by Mr. Gostock. She sipped her wine and nibbled her biscuit in the mincing manner of a cat, but with an air of perfect breeding. The other two glasses were for the American and the headmistress. Not even Mrs. Stuart was asked to join in the refreshments. With a peevish air she sat apart and was able to do as we did, that is to say, to look on.

But the age of the wine and the delicacy of the biscuits were at the time matters of no moment to me.

Miss Sinclair's affirmation had greatly increased my distress. I did not doubt but that she would keep her word and would make me shriek. I could not rid my mind of her intention. But I registered an inward promise that I would make no sound at all. By my attitude of contempt, I would affirm the enduring power of my sex. They should see that a little boy had a spirit of more mettle, if not tougher than a mere little girl.

Miss Sinclair, however, was interrupted in her sipping that she might tell weeping Clara to go on her knees by the side of the high desk, keeping her petticoats raised as before. Her drawers being still down at her heels, her swollen hinder charms were to be looked at by all the scholars. The slender twigs of the birch had traced quite a network of weals of a livid red hue gradually getting purple.

The unhappy child obeyed, sobbing in a heart-broken manner. By a refinement of cruelty, pretty Miss Sinclair went to the cupboard and took out a mirror which she placed on the ground behind Clara, telling the child to look therein at the pitiful state of her thighs. The effect of this counsel was a fresh outburst of grief.

No one, however, paid any attention to me.

I seemed to have been totally forgotten. But I noticed, on all sides, covert glances in my direction. Some of the pupils fixed a compassionate gaze upon me; but most seemed to be simply in a state of curiosity not unmixed with cruel satisfaction.

At length Miss Sinclair, the directress, and Mr. Gostock put down their empty glasses at the same moment and brushed the biscuit crumbs from their hands.

Miss Sinclair looked in my direction and raised a finger as a sign to me. The gesture was imperious. I trembled and I think I became deathly pale. The idea of disobeying did not so much as occur to me. Tottering on my hateful Louis XV heels, my feet crushed and tortured in the ridiculous raised arched boots, I drew near the table of execution. Pretty Stella had only to make a sign and with the docility of a lamb, I took the same position as Clara had done previously. That is to say, I lay upon it with my face thrust forwards and downwards, away from the executioner, and with my arms extended. Mrs. Stuart immediately caught hold of my wrists, and, in anticipation of possible resistance, knotted them together with a handkerchief. A quick hand raised my muslin skirts and drew them over my head which was thus muffled therein. My drawers were unfastened and slipped down my stupid black stockings to my dishonouring boots with their high insteps, and an unpleasant chilliness proved to me that my bare thighs were already delighting the class. I felt choked by an inexpressible feeling of shame. I was sick at heart and felt that I should never again be able to hold up my head.

I then knew for myself that terrible agony of waiting which had been endured by Clara. For I also, during a space of time which seemed to me endless, had to await the good pleasure of pretty imperious Miss Sinclair. As in the case of her first victim she addressed me in dulcet, honeyed tones, though they reached my ears strangely stifled by my petticoats. And this warning that she was about to begin threw me again into the most poignant sufferings at a moment when, owing to having waited so long, blessed insensibility had been creeping over me. I was beginning yet again to forget my horrible position when the first blow struck me across the thighs and all my fine resolutions disappeared like smoke, for I shrieked with all the strength of my lungs and cried for mercy like the veriest abject coward.

But the only response to my wails was the terrible birch, stinging like a nest of vipers.

Ah, that atrocious suffering and, more painful still, the dire humiliation! I wept, cried, shrieked, sobbed. I promised to be good and patient. I declared that not only would I never be annoyed again on account of a wretched ball of paper soaked in spittle, but that they might spit upon my face and I would not mind. The beating continued pitilessly. I threw my head from side to side and stretched my back to the right and to the left in an effort to free myself. The handkerchief which bound me enabled Mrs. Stuart to resist all my struggles.

At length, Miss Sinclair ceased whipping I had to go on my knees at the side of the table to match Clara on the other side. The mirror showed my hinder parts to be covered with blood. Nor was I permitted to leave my position there before the end of lesson time. Meantime my posterior in its wretched plight was the cynosure of every mocking pupil's eye.

CHAPTER III

With the feminine costume I acquired more and more unmistakably feminine gait. Indeed, during our playtime, for the mistress permitted us to play a few of those games popular with little girls, it would happen that should I miss a ball, I would open my legs to catch it in my skirt instead of closing my knees together to prevent the ball running through, as little boys do. Accustomed to high heels, I would walk with little prim steps, wriggling my hips.

Lady Flayskin complimented me upon the way I held myself and upon my care for my clothes.

The carriage of my head did not entirely please her. My under jaw was prominent and massive, like that of a wolf, she told me. Before being entrusted to the hands of Betsy and entering this school, I had threatened to become a real wild beast; a savage brute. I had a propensity, I may add, to thrust forward my neck like one who is ready to face friends and foes alike with equal fearlessness. This combative advance of my chin was displeasing to Lady Flayskin. Twice had she told me so. Then, for a second inattention to her words, I had been again whipped by pretty Stella before the whole assembled class, and Mr. Gostock, the friend of the directress.

But deep-seated habit was stronger than I. Whenever I was not paying special attention, my jawbone took that thrust forward familiar with boxers.

The "collar" was applied to me.

This instrument of torture consisted of a very high, thick, hard, leather collar which stretched the tendons of my neck in a manner that made me shriek with pain. It obliged me to hold my head erect. The shoulder straps were also tightened to such an extent that they pierced my flesh. The corset which they had first put on me was relatively short. They selected a longer one for my use, with steel busks incomparably stiffer, and stout Mrs. Eagle, charged specially with my dressing, pulled the laces so tight that I could scarcely breathe.

Little by little, I acquired a wasp-like waist. My boots likewise were changed. Through walking badly, I had worn out of shape those which were first given me. The new ones were far narrower and more arched. They pinched me horribly. The heels also were a good third-of-an-inch higher and very much hollowed out and pointed. If they had begun by assigning me these latter, it is certain that I should never have succeeded in making two steps without falling. Through habit, I learnt to walk like a girl. For the rest, the new boots, like the others, were sufficiently long. Though Lady Flayskin was of opinion that a boot could not be too narrow, she declared that it would be atrocious barbarity to have them too short.

This declaration was evidently regarded as sufficient for us. She took no pains to establish her subtle contention by the least argument. For that matter, I do not suppose that any reasoning would have prevented us all being afflicted with corns and bunions and our mistress was in consequence exceedingly proud.

She was equally proud of our gloves which she frequently examined, and with the minutest attention. We were punished for the least wrinkle or scratch and the only punishment employed was the whip.

It was the only recognised means of discipline. The birch was used to correct inattention and negligence. If I learnt anything at all in this establishment, it was drilled into me by the application of the birch to the proper part. It is the birch that I must thank for the little I know.

Boys and girls were treated in the same way. Our toilet was to be our chief thought and care, and since the least incorrectness in our dress was punished by a public flogging, the reader may imagine whether or no we took care to be as neat as new pins. We had to wash our hands and faces several times a day, without counting the morning bath, and although we wore our gloves continuously, we had to draw them off at least four times a day in order to show the mistress our clean hands and carefully trimmed fingernails.

As regards bodily cleanliness, Lady Flayskin's establishment could rank as a model. But the corruption of the mind brought about in this same establishment, fatal and incurable demoralisation.

This discipline by means of the corset, gloves, and whip was without pity. He who invented it was certainly vicious, but he was no fool. The net result of this treatment was the bringing into entire and abject submissiveness the most unruly disposition.

Lady Flayskin proceeded in the most methodical manner possible and step by step.

With her, boys and girls showed upright figures, incredibly slender.

Her special pride was to point to three little girls, sisters, whom their father, a widower and man of fashion, had entrusted to her keeping at a very tender age, so soon as his wife had died.

He had not desired the responsibility of bringing up three girls. They promised to become exceedingly pretty.

The eldest was ten years old; the second eight; and the youngest five. The eldest was of refined and delicate appearance, the second was round and chubby, and the youngest thin and slender. Not one of the three wore a corset when they arrived.

Lady Flayskin imposed this garment upon them from their very first day under her roof. It was not precisely a corset, but a device for moulding the bust to shape; tight-fitting, made of an unyielding material, which did not descend lower than the waist and contained no stiffeners.

In this jacket-corset, the little girls had to get through all their occupations. At night time, during their sleep, they were not permitted to take it off. They had to be content with the lacing being just loosened a little by the mistress when they went to bed.

At the end of three months, these embryonic corsets were put aside and replaced by appliances of much more serious appearance and effect. The corsets were now cut much longer, though of the same material, while whalebone stiffeners were employed and the lacing was much more tightly done by the mistress. In the evening, there was no loosening of the lacing whatever. After this garment had been employed for six months, it was replaced by what may be styled an armoured corset, yet longer than the preceding one, of stiff linen overlaid with silk, with stiffeners of steel and whalebone. The laces of plaited silk were drawn very tight. These corsets were employed for a year. They were only, it is true, used during the daytime. At night, the little girls were again dressed in their former corset, which they had worn during the preceding six months. Now, however, it was laced much more tightly and there were inserted in it some fairly yielding whalebones.

Little by little, without the apparent employment of violence, Lady Flayskin had succeeded in lacing the pupils very tightly indeed. Finally, the laces of silk were replaced by leather laces, of the material used for thongs of whips and, that the lacing might be done to perfection, a small capstan was used. The little girls had their breathing impeded and showed signs of becoming asthmatic. They complained of pains in their chests and were frightfully pale.

Lady Flayskin was pitiless. The lacing was never loosened and Nature finished by conforming to the cruelty, and the young bodies lost their pristine beauty.

These girls became exceedingly delicate; their appetite was small and their digestion impaired, while the least walking exercise took away their breath. In fact, all effort was painful.

Their waists were extraordinarily small. The plump one, whose little stomach had formerly been almost prominent, decreased in waist measure, although she had grown from a little girl to a big one. At the age of fifteen, she had chubby cheeks and large limbs, but her waist was only fifteen inches. Lady Flayskin was fond of saying with a laugh that when Miss Jessy reached her thirtieth year, her waist and her calf would measure the same in circumference.

If the other young ladies of the school were a little stouter than these three sisters whose training in the matter of corsets had been so methodical, it remained a fact that the waists of the scholars were renowned. They had a reputation which had travelled everywhere within a distance of twenty miles round, and when a young girl of remarkable smallness of waist entered a London drawing-room, the remark did not fail to be made that she must have received her education at the establishment of Lady Flayskin.

We boys were made to submit to equally severe discipline as the girls, in this matter of stays and gloves. In this extraordinary restraint, Lady Flayskin was always inflexibly severe. Sometimes she would pardon a badly-written exercise, lack of application, or chattering during class-time, but if there was so much as a crease in a glove or if a boy succeeded surreptitiously in loosening his stays to the extent of a quarter of an inch, the rod followed without mercy.

The result of thus living in a state of constraint and fear was to render our wills tractable. We became docile in the extreme, ready to submit in the most abject manner to any demand that was made of us.

We expressed our eagerness to carry out the least desire of a mistress. If Lady Flayskin herself deigned to give us an order, we obeyed with a kind of exaltation or religious terror. We all feared pretty Stella, Mr. Gostock's *protégée*, for each posterior bore lively recollections of this young lady.

This overwrought and constrained state of mind and body caused by absurd feminine garments, reduced our boyish high spirits to such a degree that we would gladly have played with dolls if we had had any. Instead of thinking of teasing the lassies, we forgot altogether that they were girls and in any way different from ourselves. This resulted from seeing so much of them, from being called by girls' names and from wearing the same clothes as they did. Similarly, when a girl was addressing me as Alice, it was hard for her to remember that I was not a girl. As girls are wont to do, we kissed and caressed one another without any wrong thoughts, yet these caresses would excite our sensibilities. We would then remember the difference of sex, though childlike we understood only vaguely the meaning of the word: *sex*. Still at such moments a feeling of fear would be aroused, and the pleasure of our sensations would be enhanced by our dread of discovery. It is true that Lady Flayskin and our mistress themselves when dressing us or flogging us would similarly excite our feelings and make us feel strangely confused. But this they never seemed to notice. They unceasingly harangued us regarding decency and morality and Mr. Gostock, who took so evident a joy in watching pretty Stella at work whipping a bare posterior, would preach most edifying sermons upon morality and chastity.

The girls' and boys' dormitories were separated, but only by a thin partition. At night, those of us boys who were not asleep would hear curious sounds. There were whisperings and kisses and the laughter of girls being tickled. Our curiosity would be awakened and we would follow suit on our side of the wall, and the girls would hear similar sounds coming from us.

It was when one of us had been whipped that the dormitory would be most astir. The others would press round the sufferer and seek to console him. At these times, we behaved like true sisters of charity. Our hands would raise the long nightgown, which as though we had been girls we all wore, and our hands would do their best by their gentle touch, to soothe the pain of the victim.

These nocturnal maraudings had their dangers, as the mistresses would frequently make their rounds. But the danger was an attraction. For — shall I confess it? — while we feared the whip, we grew to desire it. On certain days, whether because the weather was heavy or stormy, or for some other inexplicable reason, we would grow restless and commit faults with the obvious and sole object of being whipped. Sometimes Lady Flayskin, Stella, and all the mistresses were not numerous enough for the flogging which was required — our desires in this direction being always gratified to the best of the abilities of our superiors.

At these times, six boys and perhaps ten girls would be ranged in a kneeling line with drawers down, awaiting the penance of the birch.

What a chorus of cries, entreaties, sobs and wails would then be heard!

If the thick walls and the large garden had not deadened these sounds, an astonished passer-by would certainly have thought they proceeded from a madhouse. For never, unless the recollection of early days, similarly passed, had come to him, could he have guessed the truth.

CHAPTER IV

To the extent that formerly I had been playful, high-spirited and always ready to engage in pleasures and employments suited to my age and sex, so now I became reserved, secretive, and timorous. In other days, I was fond of dangerous games, cricket, bird's-nesting and suchlike. Now by chance if I saw a bird's nest at the top of a tree, and absentmindedly would imagine how easy it would be to reach it by climbing along yonder thick branch, lying the while upon my chest, extending a hand as far as this other branch or that, I would suddenly become conscious anew of my clothing. What a fine state my glazed kid gloves would be in, and my muslin petticoat, thread stockings and kid boots! The rough bark of the tree would quickly spoil the beauty of all this finery.

I do not mind owning that formerly I had been a boy fond of a good stand-up fight, though ready to forgive my foe afterwards. Now I had no pluck left. The flogging I had received the day of my arrival had taken from me any desire, at any rate for a long time afterwards, to ever avenge myself upon my schoolfellow as a healthy boy would. Instead of taking quick action, or defending myself from others with my fists, I would, like the other children, descend to cunning and slyness.

I will say no more upon this head. These recollections are very painful to me and I do not care to tell to what actions I sometimes resorted. I am now a man and ashamed of the mean actions of these childish days. As I continue this story of my youth, it is with difficulty that I can contain my anger as I think of those who were the cause of demoralisation which happily, thought no thanks to them, I have outlived.

I thought I had endured every suffering that the cruelty of Lady

Flayskin had been able to devise. Thousands of times had I cursed the corset which compressed my ribs, impeding my breathing sorely; the high heels which obliged me to take little painful, careful steps and to swing my body in a ridiculous manner; the feminine drawers, stockings and garters. I especially detested the straps which cut into my shoulders if I leant forward, and the stiff leather collar which so grievously strained my neck and prevented the least forward inclination of the head. In short, all these cruel tortures, to which no force of habit could accustom me, seemed the limit of malignant inventiveness.

I was mistaken.

In an earlier chapter I have alluded to the black kid drawers worn by Clara.

One day the directress sent for me. I went to her room with a beating heart. This summons never boded any good. It was invariably a severe reprimanding followed by a flogging sentence, or some other outrage to our childish feelings.

She began by making me a little speech in which she congratulated me upon the improvement in my conduct. She dwelt lengthily on the advantages of her system of education and asked me if I was of opinion that my bad disposition would ever have been reformed without the discipline of the corset, the high heels, and those gloves so tight that they prevented the fist being clenched when worn. As I remained mute, she frowned and repeated:

"Do you thinks so, Alice?"

"Yes, my lady."

"So you are happy here?"

"Very happy!" and I heaved a vast sigh which would have choked me had I tried to restrain it.

"You must now put this on!" she said, spreading before my eyes, which found no pleasure in the vision, a pair of those glazed kid drawers such as some of the girls and boys wore in this horrible academy.

For a minute I stood dumb and motionless, wondering if just once more I should attempt resistance. Reflecting that I should pay dearly for my folly and having before my mental vision Stella's white arm wielding a big birch-rod, I stepped forward, with an air of humble submission, took the garment, and replied:

"Certainly, my lady."

She loosened my grasp of the garment.

"No. If I had wished you to put it on later, I should have given it to Mrs. Stuart. You must put it on immediately, and I shall help you, for you would never succeed unaided. Come! Undress yourself."

Already she had loosened all my buttons with nimble fingers, and, in less time than it takes to relate, I stood before her in my chemise. The first thing I did on being freed from the corset, was to rub my back, whence the skin was slightly rasped, and which was red and sore from continual and excessive compression. This feminine gesture was a successful one! My lady condescended to one of her rare smiles. Then, unwilling to allow so excellent an opportunity for proclaiming the excellence of her establishment to escape, she said:

"Look at the proof of your change! Your movement is instinctive. You experience a sensation of irritation so soon as you remove your corset which shows that it should be taken off as seldom as possible. Let me see if you are perfectly clean."

She examined my white clean body, raising my chemise in order to be able to look at me properly. Her fingers travelled lightly over my skin and she appeared contented.

"Very good! For a boy, your skin is extraordinary. It is white and delicate. That is not merely the result of the cosmetics employed in this house, and which come, it is true, from the best perfumers of London, that your skin is so velvety. It is a natural gift and a precious one which I urge you to value. It is not usual to see so soft and feminine a skin in a member of your sex."

She bade me be seated and going upon her knees before me, began to remove my boots.

Such an attention and attitude were of evil omen and I began to feel very frightened.

When Lady Flayskin had an air of sweetness and a desire to render aid it was the sign of a fit of cold implacable wrath which was about to burst forth. She resembled the cat whose claws are sharpest and cruellest when the paw seems most soft and velvety.

I endeavoured to aid her, astonished and confused at this removal of my boots by the directress, but she pushed my hands away, saying:

"No! No! Keep quiet, will you? I tell you once for all that I do not wish for interference from my pupils. It is my desire to remove your boots; that is my whim, is it not? Do you understand?"

The look she gave me showed me plainly that it was not from humility that she performed this servile action.

When my boots had been removed, I was about to take off my long cotton stocking, but she authoritatively intervened:

"No! No! Keep them on! They will not be at all in the way."

She again took up the kid garment that she had laid upon the back of a chair, when about to undress me. It was a garment of a soft yielding appearance which appeared to me to be much too tight for my body. It was at the same time a sort of vest buttoning up at the side with mother-o'-pearl buttons, and a pair of drawers of most slender proportions.

The stockings certainly did not prove to be in the way. But after the legs of the drawers had been pulled up over my slender calves — as thin and wiry as a stag's — they refused to mount my thighs.

Lady Flayskin pulled. I stretched out my legs making them as stiff as possible. In spite of myself, I could not help bending my knees, so violent was the strain put upon them by the pulling. Then the wrathful voice of my lady made me tremble.

"Will you be so good as to sit quiet, Alice? You are behaving badly on purpose, you bad boy! If you begin again you shall taste the whip before leaving this room."

Her threat did not strengthen my powers of resistance. My legs bent again, weak with fear.

With compressed lips and furious eyes, Lady Flayskin regarded me in silence. She had abandoned her efforts. Happily for me a diversion took place at this critical moment.

A knock was heard at the door.

It was Mrs. Eagle, the stout under-mistress, leading into the room, in response to my lady's "Come in!" the three sisters, the pride of the establishment. I have already spoken of these three young ladies and of their waists, whose slenderness was due to the discipline of the corset as prescribed by Lady Flayskin.

My lady looked as them with pride and contentment. Her ill-humour immediately vanished. She forgot it at the sight of her favourite pupils and told Mrs. Eagle to see to the completion of my dressing.

The three girls, perfect mannequins as regarded their proportions, stood modestly together. The eldest was now sixteen years old, with a transparent complexion and feverish eyes. At the sight of her waist, people wondered how she could move without breaking into two pieces. Her waist was quite round and the appearance of slimness was thus accentuated. It was certainly not more than fifteen inches round. Her shoulders were lamentably narrow, but nevertheless appeared broad and finely proportioned by contrast with her slender waist.

The younger sister was my lady's triumph, the stout child who was now fifteen years of age. When first brought to the school, she seemed about to become elephantine. Her appetite however, was not unusually large. It seemed that everything she ate nourished her, turning to fat and muscle, yet Lady Flayskin showed no disposition to oppose this corpulency. She proscribed neither potatoes nor pastry, and the lass might take as much farinaceous food as she wished. I may say that as regards food, we were as well treated as the most exacting parents could have required. This was fitting in an establishment which in its way was extremely luxurious and certainly very expensive. I do not think that in the whole of England could have been found an educational establishment whose terms were higher. We certainly had excellent and abundant food, good cooking, together with encouragement to satisfy our appetites on the part of the teacher. The young lady of whom I am telling you had profited thereby. She ate everything and asked for more, being no different in this respect from some of the other pupils. Big appetites in this establishment were not exceptional, the girls being some of them as hearty eaters as the boys.

While placing no obstacle to the girl's increasing corpulency, for the neck, shoulders, arms and legs were becoming of monstrous proportions, Lady Flayskin was careful to see to the diminishing of the waist measure by the continual and judicious employment of suitable corsets.

The result was extraordinary.

It seemed impossible that this child, whose chest was compressed and whose stomach was tightly girded night and day, could digest food and continue to grow fat. Yet such was the case. Her disposition was cheerful; ever ready for a joke and a laugh, she was always a source of jesting among her companions who loved her for her gaiety. Sometimes her laughter would terminate in a painful grimace. The inexorable corset was unfavourably disposed to an excess of laughter and made its wearer pay for liberties. It refused to yield so much as half an inch. But the moment of pain would pass and the young girl would become again as lighthearted as ever.

She was of the same height as her elder sister who, as I have just related, was exceedingly tall and seemed even taller on account of her slenderness. The height of the second sister, by reason of her stoutness, appeared less remarkable. The youngest sister was as thin and tall as the eldest, but her frame was even more delicate, while a look of unspeakable sadness veiled the blue depths of her eyes.

Lady Flayskin had punished all three of them, for some childish fault or for no fault at all. Had all been guilty at the same time it would indeed have been strange. The notion of a plot was impossible in this establishment, even in the case of sisters. The discipline of the corset not only brought about a reduction of the waist but also reduced initiative and courage. No one of the girls or boys who were educated in the academy would have dared to conceal anything from the mistresses. The fear of the whip, too, was an added incentive to constant and cringing submission.

If one of the pupils had thought of carrying out some plot, no matter how innocent might have been the projected escapade, it is certain that one of those led into the secret whether boy or girl, would have done their best to swiftly master all the details in order to reveal the whole matter to one of the mistresses without delay.

Lady Flayskin, when in humour to punish, did not require a peccadillo to be necessarily committed by the selected victim. She herself imagined the fault and the victim experienced the whip. She always contrived to give an appearance of justice to her wrath. Her hypocrisy was unbounded. There was no appeal from her judgments and any attempt to gain a hearing brought added punishment as the result of such imprudence.

The three sisters stood in a row, very erect, the head well up and the neck stretched as high as possible. The leather collar which was occasionally worn by the other pupils was always worn by these three girls, except when outside the school walls, when habit enabled them to hold up their heads stiffly. They frequently went out walking and visiting and were always accompanied by Lady Flayskin herself. I learnt the meaning of these exhibitions later. The four of them would go to parties in the best London society. Apart from ladies of the most aristocratic exclusiveness, there would be politicians of grave and austere mien, merchant princes, judges, all men of note and position, and they would, men or women alike, behave to these unfortunate girls with nameless barbarity. These people were the friends of the directress of the school. Beneath an exterior of austere morality, all concealed the most vicious instincts. After an elegant dinner, followed by some equally good music or perhaps by a dance, in fact after an evening spent in a fashion customary in all good society, an orgy ensued. This would begin by admiring the "Wasps," as the sisters were called on account of the extraordinary smallness of their waists. Conversation regarding their figures would follow. Then a desire would be expressed to see and handle. After many apparent refusals, Lady Flayskin, liking people to beg her favours, and who wished to make the projected entertainment last longer, would tell the girls to undress. The men would then exert their biceps to the utmost and would endeavour to lace the stays yet tighter. If, as almost invariably happened, the girls fainted, the whip would arouse them from their swoon.

At the moment of which I am writing, they were doing their best to smile at Lady Flayskin whose pleasure they were awaiting.

The directress, preferring to leave them in the distress of their uncertainty, turned to me and found me toiling with the nameless "combination" which was at the same time drawers and jacket, of kid throughout.

Mrs. Eagle was employing all her strength in the attempt to make the legs of the drawers mount my thighs. The savage fingers of this stout woman pinched the leather and me indifferently. I cried. Lady Flayskin looked at me tenderly and I began to sob. Whether purposely, as is more probable, or through carelessness, these abominable drawers had been made a great deal too tight. It is true my gloves were tight also. They yielded a little, though far from sufficiently for comfort. As to Mrs. Eagle, that lady was as red as a tomato and perspired and puffed while becoming more impatient. Nor were her feelings calmed by Lady Flayskin who watched her with compressed lips and who twice or thrice had coldly remarked:

"Not like that! Ah! my poor Mrs Eagle, I thought you had more skill!"

The under-mistress, irritated by observations to which she dared not reply, continued her efforts with even more violence and avenged herself on my skin. Her thick, strong fingers would seize and pinch a piece of my skin without pity, while I had to do my utmost to make no sound.

With eyes dilated by pain, I followed the progress of the wretched garment which, in spite of all difficulties, was actually beginning to climb my thighs like a thick black snake.

At last, it was accomplished! The sensation of being so compressed was far from agreeable. They had even been obliged to powder the interior of the garment to permit it to be drawn over my body, clammy with pain and fear. It was now only a question of buttoning the jacket. It was fastened diagonally by mother-o'-pearl buttons which began at the left shoulder and ended at the right hip. It was an even more difficult matter than the fastening of the drawers and infinitely more painful. The fixing of the very first button was terrible. My skin had become caught between the button and the button-hole, and in spite of this, the malicious fingers of Mrs. Eagle did their best to complete the buttoning, skin and all. I writhed with pain and she had to struggle anew at her task, though not before administering me a vigorous thump on my head with her heavy hand. I began to moan and weep softly.

Lady Flayskin again intervened.

"Why do you strike him?"

"He uses all his efforts to get away. The button was just going in when he shifted again, little brute that he is! It's no easy task to dress such a child."

"Because you are clumsy, I repeat. Since he shows a disposition to resist you, his new drawers shall be christened by a good flogging with the horsewhip."

I joined my hands together and burst into sobs. Hitherto I had only been birched. The horsewhip appeared much more horrible.

Lady Flayskin took no notice of my pantomime of despair. She merely thrust Mrs. Eagle aside and remarked coldly:

"Give me your place. As you are unable to dress him I will do it myself."

The under-mistress did not dare to make the least objection, but she gave me a covert glance of malice which boded ill for me as soon as I should be again alone with her.

Lady Flayskin had not been incorrect in styling the under-mistress as clumsy. She herself made proof of incredible dexterity.

Seizing the button firmly, she put it into the button-hole without pinching my skin at all. Still the pain she gave me was extreme. She had no thought for my feelings as she compressed my little chest and I could scarcely breathe. It seemed to me that my sufferings would never end except at the expense of crushed ribs. Fear of the whip, however, made me control my feelings as well as I could, although I had but faint hopes of being let off the promised punishment.

Meanwhile the young ladies with their wasp-like waists had undressed in accordance with the order given them by terrible Lady Flayskin.

They had first of all drawn off their long, black kid gloves, hanging them with extreme care upon the backs of their chairs, in such a way that no pair hung lower than another by so much as a fraction of an inch. To this points the directress, who attached extreme importance to details, paid vigilant attention. Then, still in an orderly methodical manner, they had taken off their dresses. This was an easy matter, but it was otherwise when the corset had to be removed, a terrible and painful undertaking. The three unfortunate girls had their stomachs so compressed that it was impossible to make them recede farther. To take off their corsets appeared to be a task even more beyond their powers than that of putting them on. The stiffening whalebones appeared inseparable from their flesh, and it seemed impossible to remove the stays without at the same time removing the skin of the wearers. With heads thrown back, pale as death, they struggled until their active fingers became numbed and for just a moment, they paused. The cutting voice of Lady Flayskin immediately reproved their idleness. They therefore recommenced their seemingly impossible task. At length, one of them succeeded in undoing a hook and the corset at once came together yet tighter at the top, compressing her breasts with such violence that overcome by her sufferings she almost fell to the ground. She continued her efforts in spite of all, eager to gain a little respite from the awful compression, even at the expense of the whipping which the directress had announced would follow the performance of her task. At length, with a groaning sigh, she managed to detach the corset entirely from her body. She held it at arm's length and with the other hand, she energetically rubbed her back to relieve the unendurable irritation.

All three were now undressed. Their sumptuous clothes were laid out in orderly fashion and each pair of boots was placed neatly in front of a chair. I was stupefied at the sight of those boots. My own, at which I had so bitterly grumbled, were not to be compared with these. Their tips were varnished and the leather was picked out in white stitching which showed up effectively on the dark ground. The heels were, of course, very high, and cut away to an extraordinary extent. Indeed the foot when encased seemed almost in a line with the leg. The length, however, of the boots was exaggerated and the toes tapered to a very small point. They mounted high up the leg, as far as the calf which in these three young ladies was situated very high up. This is, I am told, an undoubted sign of aristocratic birth.

Whether aristocratic or not, the lines of their figures were very graceful, and perhaps this was entirely due to the efforts of Lady Flayskin.

Young as I was, and incompetent therefore to criticise feminine beauty, these excessively slender waists struck me as ridiculous, more especially in the case of the second sister whose body filled and stretched her "combination" almost to bursting point. She was a perfect ball of a girl. Her breasts were large and naturally very firm, for she was fifteen years old. Her stomach, freed now from the compression of the corset, but squeezed by the leather garment, was nevertheless able to take its natural somewhat protruding position. In short, her general appearance with her large shoulders and arms, as big as those of Mrs. Eagle, her thick legs and thighs and swelling calves, formed a striking contrast with the small narrow waist, the latter seeming to be a slender isthmus uniting the two voluminous peninsulas of the breast and the vast fat chest with the monstrous hinder parts and hips.

It is to be supposed that Lady Flayskin's opinion and my own were not the same on this subject, and I was careful not to express my thoughts aloud.

I am of this opinion because I noticed the look of satisfaction bestowed by the head mistress upon the three young ladies now clothed so summarily in their tight-fitting black kid combinations. Possibly the mistress's eye shone most as it surveyed the stout chubby cheeked girl who formed such a contrast with her slender sisters.

They stood in a row, as modestly as they could, although the scanty nature of their costume was such as to reveal with a near approach to indecency, rather than to conceal the exact shape of the lassies wearing it. They awaited the pleasure of their directress who was occupied in martyrising me by buttoning the horrible combination. She did not spare me a single button's agony.

At length her task was completed. The horrible garment was buttoned up. Its coldness struck ice into my bones; it seemed to choke my heart and lungs struggling vainly to resist the attack upon their natural freedom.

It is needless to enquire if I was in dire distress. I suffered even more in mind than in body. The directress ordered me to remove my stockings and my pains were increased, for upon trying to lean forward to obey her, this leather corset, at once so supple and so inflexible, resisted all my efforts. I stooped to the right and then to the left with no more success in one direction than in another.

Fear intensified my discomfort, as the directress laughed, watching my sterile efforts to obey her.

Being unable to lean forward, I tried to go on my knees.

The horrible tightness of the drawers impeded all movements. My back seemed paralysed and I had the notion, no doubt only imaginary, that the garment was splitting.

If it had really split, how terrible would have been my punishment!

At last, moving my arms in order to ease my shoulders, I succeeded in making these stockings, which I was told to remove, descend a little way. Seeing then clearly that I should never succeed in my task by the employment of hands alone, I adopted another method. I put one foot upon the other, and then by with drawing the one which was beneath, endeavoured to pull off the stocking at the same time.

The directress said nothing on seeing my fresh device for doing her bidding, but took up a heavy horsewhip from the mantelpiece.

At that moment, though I do not know how I contrived it, I succeeded in raising one foot up to the height of my hand on the same side, and in grasping and removing the stocking; and, as by miracle, I succeeded with the other stocking too.

My costume was now exactly similar to that of the three young ladies, for I wore nothing but the ridiculous combination, formed of a single piece. Chest and thighs were bare, stained with the black of the glazed kid which had effectually left its mark upon my white skin.

But I differed from the girls in having my hair cut short. I was not so very different in general appearance from the eldest and the youngest whose bodies were thin and extremely unpronounced in outline except as regards the waist. On the other hand, I in no way resembled the second sister whose bulging, enormous proportions would have filled the room had her garment given way.

The directress now examined us at length, measuring and weighing us, and noting the circumference of our waists. The result of her examination she carefully inscribed in a notebook she kept for that purpose.

Then she announced that we now had to submit to the punishment we had merited.

Brandishing the horsewhip with an air of inexorable decision, she took hold of the eldest girl by the nape of the neck and thrust her down on her knees. The girl's thin hinder parts stretched the drawers so tight that not a wrinkle showed. Then the whip descended with sound and fury, the mistress paying no heed to cries, protestations, and tears of agony.

It was next the turn of the second sister to bend tight her kid-covered vast posterior to the terrible whip, and then the youngest submitted to the same penalty.

My turn arrived only too quickly.

The pain of the application of the rod was even more terrible than those moral agonies I had gone through while awaiting it. Still crying out with the pain, I had then to dress again with all haste in my girlish clothes, not forgetting the boots, under penalty of receiving a supplementary dose of the birch.[1]

---

[1] The author of this work would be pleased to receive any manuscripts, documents, etc., relating to corporal punishment or discipline, for his private collection. Novels to order.

Apply, by letter only, to billet Chamonix, 592, Bureau restant, n° 1, Paris.

CHAPTER V

I have lately learnt that the Chinese deform their women's feet for purely voluptuous reasons.

The steps taken in walking being by this means made very short and stiff, the reaction exhibits itself in extraordinary suppleness in the swinging movements of the hips and back, excellent training, in the opinion of the Chinese, for the lists of love. The calves also become emaciated to a certain extent, but to the profit of the thighs. The latter grow fat and firm as also the spherical parts below the loins.

I was struck by this explanation because it enabled me to regard the western high heel habit, from another point of view. The woman's or girl's foot is compelled by the height of a very lofty heel to take an almost vertical position. The resulting swinging of the hips and the little play given to the calves, are similar to what is noted in the case of the ladies of the Celestial Empire.

The discomfort caused by the high-heeled boots, the long tight-fitting gloves and the cruel corset, above all the terror in which we lived of the birch, all this kept us in a continual state of nervous excitement, which easily transformed itself into eroticism and unhealthy passions. The dormitories never echoed with such hysterical laughter of little girls, nor such loud and pealing laughter of others, nor such deep-drawn sighs, as upon those days when whipping had been most general.

Above all our physical distress inspired us with a religious terror of our head-mistress, and a morbid desire to be obedient which brought us to a state of high excitement at the least order from her mouth.

On receiving an order from Lady Flayskin, our nerves became highly strained and we experienced a fever of voluptuous longing with a burning desire to gratify our feelings.

Never, however, could I have imagined so complete an illustration of the success of Lady Flayskin's system of education as that embodied in the person of Miss Virginia Malville.

This young lady was heiress to one of the proudest titles of old England and daughter of a peer. Her education had been deplorably neglected by an indulgent mother.

Miss Virginia had reached her eighteenth year at the time of her mother's sudden death.

Lord Malville paid the proper tribute of tears and mourning to his deceased wife and then thought that it was high time to subdue the haughty temper of his daughter, otherwise the latter would give him trouble of a serious nature later on. In any case, Lord Malville, as an upright man, accounted the marriage portion which he should bestow an insufficient compensation to a future husband for the temper of the wife. A violent husband would certainly strangle her, while she would have rendered the life of a feeble mate ridiculous in a thousand ways, and have made him the slave of every whim.

One beautiful May morning in 1896, a superb victoria and pair made a sensation at the establishment of Lady Flayskin. It drew up before the door and the directress went herself to meet it. We felt sure that the people in the carriage must be of very great distinction and we did not change this first impression upon seeing Lord Malville alight.

He was a man of from forty-five to fifty years of age, tall and erect, with regular features and as carefully shaved of all moustache or whisker as an actor.

After gravely alighting, Lord Malville turned to hand his daughter out.

Miss Virginia was tall and handsome, and carried herself like a queen or a goddess. When the eyes of this divinity rested upon us, we were able to read clearly therein that we were accounted as of no importance. Never have I seen in such beautiful eyes so tranquil an expression of contempt for the generality of mankind. To the low bow of the directress, she replied politely, nothing more, and in a way which appeared to me as impertinent as in fact it really was.

I understood Lady Flayskin's smile as she raised her head again.

Such a smile was of ill augury. Doubtless she was already planning her revenge.

It is unnecessary to say that we were not admitted to the drawing-room during the interview which immediately followed between Lord Malville, beautiful Virginia, and the directress. Nor have I ever since heard what transpired. We were, however, able to employ our imagination to good purpose through the subsequent course of events and their apparent connection with this interview.

From what we could learn from the servants, Lord Malville did justice to the luncheon offered to him and his daughter by the directress, and on taking leave of Lady Flayskin, he remarked — his heightened complexion showing that he had drunk several generous bumpers of old claret:

"It is understood! Make my daughter into as accomplished a lady as you are yourself, if possible. I give you *carte blanche*."

After his departure, Lady Flayskin introduced Miss Virginia Malville to the class over which Mrs. Stuart presided.

I have hitherto omitted to state that this curious establishment had but one class. This fact did not prevent the pupils from pursuing their course of study in an otherwise normal manner, for each boy and girl was taken separately, even if only for a few minutes, in his lesson. Application and diligence did the rest. No one was idle, so genuine was the fear inspired by corset and whip.

Of the two latter incentives to good conduct, Miss Virginia had hitherto lived in ignorance, nor was it in keeping with the traditions of the establishment that Lady Flayskin should have introduced the girl to her classmates, without having previously obliged her to don the school uniform: white muslin dress with azure-blue silk sash, high-heeled, high-topped boots and the pitilessly tight corset which robbed its wearer of the power to breathe in comfort. Clearly the directress meditated a plan.

The greatest attention was paid to the newcomer by both the mistresses. Miss Virginia, in her rich silk frock, cut a very creditable figure among the pupils. Her waist, it is true, was not so small as theirs, but it was slender and her general bearing showed grace and health.

The directress mounted her high desk, and after a few more

words in the same tone of affection to Miss Virginia, left the room.

The new girl's desk was situated near the gangway which, as I have already mentioned, divided the girls from the boys. Her seat was just facing my own, or rather, our two desks were separated from each other by the gangway.

Miss Virginia appeared at first to listen with attention to Mrs. Stuart's lecture upon the manners of good society, the necessity of men showing refinement both in their words and acts and acquiring such culture by carefully training themselves and weighing the importance of trifles, together with the duty of women to show themselves correct in manner and pretty. This gave occasion for her to explain the usefulness of the discipline of the corset and of high heels in breaking the unruly tempers of children and giving them that dignity of bearing of which later they would be so gladly proud.

Mrs. Stuart discoursed at great length upon this favourite subject of which our ears grew weary in this dread college. The angular mistress's speeches were tiresome. She loved repetition and was an orator whose great power consisted in the ability to weary her hearers.

Miss Virginia had listened at first, but she soon took up a book and became absorbed in its pages, but not for long. She yawned nervously and, through making a sudden movement, let drop the paper-knife she was holding. It fell near my own desk.

Either because she thought it beneath her dignity to cross the gangway and pick up the object herself, or because she regarded me as an inferior, although I do not think she suspected my sex, or for some other reason which I do not know, she looked at me and made the sound:

"Pst! Pst!"

I only paid more complete attention to the lecture of Mrs. Stuart, having no notion whatever of risking punishment in order to oblige the newcomer whose grand air I found insupportable.

She continued:

"Pst! Pst!"

With instinctive impatience, I shrugged my shoulders. Then without dropping her voice appreciably, she said to me:

"Here! You! Little girl! Pick up my paper knife."

I imprudently replied:

"Pick it up yourself! I am not your valet!"

"Valet?" said she in a tone of surprise. "You mean lady's maid?"

"I said what I meant to say. Leave me alone!"

And I tossed my head as I had had the habit of doing when still a boy and anxious to show my resolution in anything I decided to do.

Mrs. Stuart listened to this dialogue in a kind of stupor, for it was conducted almost in ordinary tones, forming an extraordinary interruption to the usual studious tranquillity of the class. Evidently she had heard every word, for Miss Virginia's tones were even more raised than my own, and she was aware that it was the newcomer who had first broken the silence by her "Pst! Pst!" so annoying to listen to, but replied to by me first of all by a mere shrug of the shoulders, as I had only given a direct reply after being addressed directly and in a most insulting manner.

Mrs. Stuart was well aware of the circumstances, nor for the moment was she otherwise than impartial, for she merely turned to Mrs. Eagle who was standing by the wall keeping watch over our behaviour in a majestic manner:

"Kindly inform our gracious Lady Flayskin that her presence is requisite here," said Mrs. Stuart.

The directress entered the room a moment later.

I was confident of the justice of my cause although greatly excited. My distress may therefore be imagined when I heard that horrid old fishwife Mrs. Stuart, give the affair quite a different colouring.

From her maliciously concocted version it appeared that I was the chief culprit, and the directress was obliged even to gather from this fallacious account that I was the only guilty party.

I was a young, loyal-hearted boy and at a complete loss to understand this feminine perfidy. It was clear that a victim was required. Unkind fate had designed me for the part. The unfortunate sitting part of my body was to pay the cost of Miss Virginia's first lesson.

As to the second lesson... But I will not anticipate.

"Alice!" said the directress. "Come here!"

My feeling of the injustice of this treatment was for me the strongest and uppermost feeling of my mind at that moment. Two months of discipline by means of chastisement and all these instruments of feminine toilet had not yet entirely extinguished my old instincts of rebellion. I was not yet sufficiently cowed. My fiery temperament gained the better of me and I cried out:

"In the first place my name is not Alice. It is ridiculous so to call me. I am a boy, my name is Jimmy. As for that girl there..."

I pointed with a finger over my shoulder, indicating the newcomer without deigning to look at her.

"She need not show off her grand airs with me, for they lose their effect. I told her that I was not her valet and that was what I meant to tell her. Why do you say nothing to her? It is she who began."

Little stifled laughs in the class-room proved to me that I had won a triumph, of which, in point of fact, I had no great reason to be proud. None the less, I had my moment of pride. I was not wearing the leather collar, so I bent my head, thrusting forward my chin in the attitude dear to boxers. I think, (may heaven forgive me if I am mistaken!) that I even struck an attitude of pugilistic defence, or almost did so, for my courage did not permit me to complete the gesture. What I did was to clench my fists as much as my gloves permitted and to hold out my bent elbow and forearm in front of any chest.

"Alice," repeated Lady Flayskin, "come here!"

My courage gave way on perceiving the contraction of her brows. I went forward in a state of pitiful fear, my hands up to my face, weeping hot tears, crying with anger in spite of my fear. I think I stumbled slightly by reason of my high heels.

"Go and find me the whip, Stella! The strongest of all! You know which I mean! That African whip ending in a piece of solid hippopotamus leather.

"You will find it in the second of the lowest drawers of my secretary. Here is the key!"

Pretty Stella, with a hateful smile, went swiftly to obey. The directress then turned to me.

"Undress yourself!"

I cried and wept but took everything off, laying each garment upon my chair, until I only had on the hideous glazed kid combination which gave me the appearance of having a negro's body and legs, so black and shiny looking was I.

Still bemoaning my fate, I went on my knees at the feet of the pitiless directress and with clasped hands entreated her to pardon me. She let me speak without showing the least sign either of pity or impatience. No hope could live in the face of this impassibility and I had a fit of sobbing, my grief knowing no bounds when I saw Stella appear bringing the hideous lash.

It was formed of one single piece of leather and was perfectly round. The handle end was twice as thick as the thumb, but the whip tapered gradually to the extreme end where it became a thin quivering cat's tail, or, to describe it better, the tail of a venomous serpent. The wooden handle however, was always rigid.

At the idea that my wretched rump was about to be beaten with this implement, I became mad with terror and finding no words having power to excite Lady Flayskin's pity, I clasped my hands in despairing entreaty.

The ogress could only furnish me with the following consoling words:

"Take off your drawers immediately!"

I was stupefied. Apart from the consideration that it was no small affair to remove my drawers which stuck to my skin, my hands were in such a state of trembling that I found the task of even added difficulty. Besides, it was impossible to remove the drawers without taking off the whole combination, the two parts of this garment being joined together.

I was thus asked to strip myself entirely naked before the assembled scholars and this terrible instrument was about to be used upon me behind. I was, I meditated, going to be beaten to death.

I cried, struggled, thought of trying to escape. But I was already in the grip of angular Mrs. Stuart and rotund Mrs. Eagle. The thin woman quickly unbuttoned the vest with her wiry fingers, not omitting to cruelly pinch my flesh, and the fat one inflicted upon me an equal martyrdom as she made the drawers, far too tight, descend my thighs.

I quickly found myself entirely naked and exposed to the looks of curiosity or amusement of the whole school.

No one, however, ventured to make a remark, save Miss Virginia, who, at a moment when my hysterical sobs were becoming more controlled, cried out disdainfully:

"Why it's a boy!"

Terrible Lady Flayskin, with wrath depicted upon her countenance, turned upon the owner of the voice:

"I beg you to be silent, Miss. No talking is permitted during school- hours."

"Ah! How curious!"

"I beg you to be quiet!"

"Certainly, madam."

The lofty young lady had risen and was preparing to quit the room. The directress again addressed her:

"Where are you going?"

"To my room."

"You have no room. You sleep in the dormitory, like the rest of the pupils."

"I understand perfectly, but neither of bedroom nor of dormitory shall I make any use."

"Really?"

"Yes, really."

"Would you be so kind as to inform me of the reason of this decision? I should be interested to hear it."

"Greatly interested?"

"Greatly interested."

"Very well then, I will satisfy your curiosity."

"You are indeed condescending."

"I am!"

"Speak, Miss! Speak! or if not..." said the irritable directress grinding her teeth.

"Or, if not?"

"Will you speak?"

"Drop that tone, I beg you, my lady. You appear to be ignorant of the quality of the person with whom you are speaking. I desire neither bedroom nor dormitory because I intend to leave your house. I shall not remain an instant longer than is necessary under the same roof as a person who has dared to treat me with the disrespect you are at present exhibiting towards me."

The directress, by one of those efforts of the will with which we were familiar, suddenly calmed herself. By the movement of her nostrils and her extreme pallor we knew that this calm was only affected. Her wrath was increasing inwardly.

"We will renew this conversation presently with your permission, Miss. Meanwhile, will you sit down again in your place and witness the punishment of this little boy whose insolence towards you merits condign chastisement?"

Miss Virginia shrugged her shoulders disdainfully as though to say that I was really a person of too little importance to have been capable of giving offence to so notable and distinguished a young lady as herself.

Nevertheless, without a further word she sat down again, curiosity depicted upon her face, hoping clearly to get some amusement at my expense. Cruelty finds its insidious way easily enough into the hearts of both girls and boys, men and women, when someone is about to be whipped.

That someone was myself. And I beg you to believe that all curiosity was banished from my heart. Terror alone inspired me. There was no place left for any other feeling.

Each mistress took hold of one of my arms and I was thus drawn to the table. Meantime officious Stella pushed me along with her two pretty hands on my stern. I tried to bite. I kicked. The two mistresses were obliged to seize me by the ears like a calf about to be slaughtered. Nimble Stella easily avoided my kicks and pinched what she held.

In this way, they succeeded in extending me upon the table. Mrs. Eagle obtained hold of my right hand and Mrs. Stuart of the left. I was laid upon the edge of the table, my feet just touching the ground. In this position, my unfortunate behind presented an admirable target for the terrible thong which Lady Flayskin was already brandishing menacingly. In her hand, the whip appeared a living thing, a horrible animal, a loathsome reptile ready to sting and bite.

I saw the scourge by looking sideways in a confused way, for my whole preoccupation at that moment was to watch the instrument of torture and not let it escape my view.

In vain already I had lost sight of it, as the directress placed herself behind me where I could not see anything. In accordance with her custom, she began to lecture me:

"You see that you have again merited punishment. I had hoped that the stays, high heels and tight gloves, would have sufficed to correct your naughtiness and thoughtlessness, I have been forced to have recourse to birch and whip. You have entreated for pity and you promised to be good in the future, but you have broken your promise. I have made you wear kid drawers, very tight and narrow, and I have tightened your stays in the hope of thus succeeding in curbing your unruly disposition. To-day you have failed to respect a young lady of noble family, and that upon the very day of her arrival among us. You have aggravated your guilt by your impertinence. This proves to me that your discipline is far from being completed yet awhile and I am obliged to give you severe punishment by means of this whip which, as you will find, is no mere toy. Do you own now that you deserve to be punished?"

"Pardon, my lady!"

"I am asking you to own your guilt."

"Pardon me! I implore you, most gracious Lady Flayskin! Have pity! Pardon me!"

"This request for pardon is a confession of guilt. I command you to be precise. Yes or no, have you deserved to be pitilessly beaten?"

"Oh!"

"Will you reply by yes or by no?"

"Pity me, I entreat you!"

At this point a terrible blow cut my back parts. I struggled, foaming at the mouth, but the arms of the mistresses firmly clenched my wrists. I uttered a terrible cry and shrieked:

"Yes! Yes!"

"Yes! What?"

"Yes!... Oh! No! No! I entreat you! It is too much... It will kill me!"

A second and more violent blow made me shriek out and what I had meant to say was choked by my sobs.

"I am awaiting your confession!" again said the cruel directress.

"Yes! Oh! Yes... I have deserved... I have deserved very heavy punishment... But not... Oh! No! Pity me! I entreat you!"

"I shall pity you when you have been well whipped. You shall not leave this room except with your behind streaming with blood. I give you my word, your impertinent backside shall pay for your misdeeds! Never have I seen such impertinent hindquarters! They seem to be mocking me. We shall see if they will not presently assume a more pitiful appearance. To-day I have an irresistible desire to administer a sound flogging. You have made me angry and it is necessary that my anger shall pass off."

All the time she was speaking, I had groaned and sighed ceaselessly, for the two blows she had given me seemed the acme of suffering. Nevertheless, as I was to discover, the blows were as nothing in comparison with those which were to follow.

This cruel woman who delighted to play with her victims as a cat plays with a mouse, now asked me:

"Do you promise to amend your ways and to behave better in the future?"

"Yes! Certainly!... I will never... never again..."

Here a big sob cut short my words.

"Is your repentance sincere?"

"Oh, yes!... Have pity on me, my lady!"

"No! I will have no pity! It is for your good that I punish you. I have assumed a heavy responsibility in promising to curb your unruliness which seems to defy correction. But I tell you that I will correct you! I intend you to remember this day. I intend to write this date with this lash upon your back parts in letters which shall never be obliterated. It is necessary that you carry the marks of this day's punishment as long as you live."

My teeth chattered with terror and I was still imploring for mercy in faint tones when the real whipping began.

Action followed threats so speedily that mental anguish immediately disappeared, to give place to the physical sensation of unspeakable suffering.

A rump which has not been whipped by a thong of hippopotamus hide does not know what the lash really is. No words can describe this torture. The Russian knout cannot be more barbarous.

I had no strength left to cry out, but hoarse indistinct groans came from my agonised body. Each blow found its echo in my heart which seemed on the point of bursting through excess of suffering.

The directress, with a cruelty which I can only describe as infernal, struck her blows slowly, at intervals. I listened as in a dream to Stella's sweet voice. It was her task to count the blows. This gave me no comfort, for I did not know to what number the blows were destined to amount. I listened also to the dull thud of the lash on my flesh. It was a sound like a cataract of water and filled my ears with its resounding echo. I do not think that Niagara itself can make more noise than did that lash.

The directress, after striking from left to right, struck from right to left, and the punishment ceased with a well-aimed blow, more rigorous than the others, which cut deeply into both halves of my posterior.

It seems that I received a dozen blows, including the two little preparatory ones. I could have sworn that I received more than a hundred. It is certain that if Lady Flayskin had punished me in anger, the effects would have been terrible indeed and the issue probably fatal.

Happily for me, I had simply served as an example, the real anger of the directress having for its object another person altogether, as the reader will see.

As for me, I panted; it was all that was left for me to do. The energetic attentions of the two mistresses and the salts they held to my nose brought my breath back to me. I noticed also that they touched me in a curious way with a view to restoring life in me.

The first thing I naturally proceeded to do was to set up a mournful wailing.

This did not suit the directress. It was necessary that the lesson should profit the victim, so that the example should bear fruit.

A mirror was brought and placed behind me. I looked therein with tear-dimmed eyes.

Great heavens! I was hardly able to believe in such depths of human cruelty when my eyes saw, reflected from the polished surface of the mirror, my unfortunate back parts furrowed by livid weals, my flesh divided, so to speak, into a number of lumps whence the blood trickled in little streamlets down my thighs.

A kind of delirium seized me. I called for my dear mother in piercing shrieks. Two maid-servants at once hurried in, replying to the electric bell. I was carried away in their arms, out of the school-room. They laid me on my belly, as it was not possible to think of putting me upon my back. After applying vaseline to my thighs — though it seemed to me that I was being touched with red-hot iron bars — the compassionate maids did their best in every way to relieve my sufferings. They tried to tempt me with dainties for which I had not the least appetite. Then, better inspired, remarking the condition of nervous excitement into which the terror and suffering of my whipping had thrown me, their hands softly caressed me and calmed my poor body. The state of stupor which resulted enabled me to fall asleep. But my slumbers were feverish, disturbed by nightmares.

I learnt later from my companions what had happened in the class-room after I had been carried out.

To tell the truth, I regretted savagely that I had been unable to be present during that memorable scene. Every detail, however, was so minutely described to me subsequently that I was able to conjure up the picture perfectly. I think that the description I received and which I shall now reproduce, will enable the reader to have the whole scene clearly before his eyes.

Scarcely was I outside the door of the class room, whence almost fainting I was carried by the strong arms of the maid-servants, when Lady Flayskin advanced to Miss Virginia, stopping before her and crossing her arms on her chest. She still held in her hand the terrible lash, and laughed harshly as she remarked:

"It is our turn now, Miss!"

"What do you mean?" replied the noble young lady, keeping countenance very well although her colour began to fade.

"I mean that you are about to immediately undress yourself in order that I may flog you before the whole class with the whip you are looking at. I shall lash you more severely than that urchin who, after all, was much less to blame than you."

"What is the meaning of this foolish jest?" said the young girl, withdrawing a step from the directress.

"As to folly, you are the only fool here, so remember that once for all!"

This was too much for the rich heiress of a family of knights and nobles. The colour rose to her cheeks, as with imperious voice and authoritative glance, she cried:

"Never have I been addressed in the least accent or tone of disrespect! How do you, ignoble creature, dare to be so audacious? To have imagined the possibility of my taking off my clothes before this assemblage of scholars, constitutes a criminal offence. But your most odious proceeding is to have dared to threaten me with the whip. I have told you that I wish to quit this establishment. Allow me to pass. I warn you that if you have the temerity to lay so much as a finger upon me I shall make you bitterly repent it. You and your like are made to serve upon their knees women of my rank and position."

The sardonic laugh of Lady Flayskin made the pupils tremble. She replied: "Very well! Then I will be your servant. But it is you who will be on bended knees. Come here without further delay!"

The imperious directress pointed with extended finger to the place I had just left. With the other arm she brandished the whip which whistled horribly in the air. Her features took on terrible beauty like that of a Nemesis of old.

In reply, Miss Virginia turned her back and deliberately walked towards the door, with the obvious intention of leaving the room and perhaps the house also. Scarcely had she opened the door, than she tottered backwards and was hurled irresistibly into the centre of the room. Two of the strongest maid-servants of the establishment had been informed by Stella of what was happening, and in accordance with the orders they received, had been awaiting the signal of Lady Flayskin to burst into the room and lay strong hands on Miss Virginia and prevent her from quitting the premises.

They thrust back the young girl and then seized her by the shoulders and pulled her along.

The maid-servants were followed into the room by Mr. Gostock. It had clearly been Stella who had summoned the gentleman at the psychological moment, possibly with the cognisance of the directress who always was indulgent with the Puritan Yankee.

He did not conceal his sentiments towards pretty Stella. With visible pleasure, he caressed her hand, then softly stroked the girl's chin. These trivial gestures on the part of so austere and grave a man did not fail to amaze the entire school.

Miss Virginia, who had thus been forcibly thrust back into the room by the servants, had recovered from her first astonishment. This tall strong girl, whose muscles were in excellent trim owing to her athletic training, for she had been brought up to play all open-air games and indulge in all those sports so much in vogue among English girls of the highest rank, had energetically resisted her assailants. But she had to do with those who were stronger than she herself. The two servants were Welsh, and had been carefully selected by the astute directress from among the most thickset and muscular of their race. They were two tall, heavy-limbed country wenches, square waisted and animal-faced, showing in every feature obstinate resolution and brutality. They wore neither gloves, stays, nor high heels. Their movements were easy. They were, in fact, primitive beings, true savages, or, to describe them otherwise, strong and ferocious watchdogs who obeyed their mistress's voice only, growling and gnashing their teeth at every other person so ill-advised as to think of giving them an order.

These women found amusement in the resistance offered by Miss Virginia, and they burst into unintelligent peals of laughter as they showed the muscles of their big arms and did what they liked with the elegant and disdainful young lady, treating her as though she had been a mere bundle.

While Miss Virginia struggled vainly against her robust guardians, who held her much as dogs hold a wild boar they have run down, she cried out to the directress in a hoarse voice:

"Infamous woman, will you be so good as immediately to order these low mercenaries to remove from my noble body their hands inured to servile tasks?"

The directress replied:

"Don't use such fine phrases!"

"Know this!" continued Virginia with difficulty, for she was almost too short of breath to speak. "For all these outrages, my father will wreak terrible vengeance. You will have an account to pay to the law, my lady, for your acts of violence which are not permitted by the laws of this country to its citizens."

"When women have political rights, Miss, you will be a most suitable person to head the list of the candidates for an election to Parliament. You speak with great facility and were it not that my servants are holding you most tightly, you would speak even more effectively. In a meeting you would gain great and deserved success. But until that time arrives we must exercise patience, and while awaiting it, prepare to be whipped."

"What? What? You persist in your execrable plan? You would dare to lay the whip upon the descendant of one of the noblest families of England? You think of imposing upon me, Miss Virginia Malville, a punishment which would brand me with disgrace! Do you mean me?"

"Yes, you! Punishment will begin immediately."

"I repeat that you have reason to fear my father. His vengeance will be implacable."

"Thank you for the care you evidently take of my interests. But I am able to reassure you. Listen while I read this."

While the servants held the haughty young lady by her wrists and shoulders, the directress, standing in front of her, unfolded a sheet of paper and read out an authorisation duly delivered to her by Lord Malville. The nobleman declared in this document "that he was weary of the headstrong will and capriciousness of his daughter, and that not only he himself but the young lady's governesses and professors were also out of patience. That, for these reasons, he, the noble lord, handed over his daughter to the good keeping of Lady Flayskin. That he empowered the said Lady Flayskin to take entire control of his daughter and to employ all such means and methods of discipline and coercion as she the said Lady Flayskin, should judge suitable with a view to the attainment of the ends proposed."

Signed: LORD REGINALD MALVILLE.

"Do you recognize the signature of the noble lord, you father?" said the directress, placing the paper under the eyes of Virginia who remained imprisoned between her two custodians.

It was impossible to deny the signature, and this it was which clearly put the young girl completely out of countenance. She reddened with shame; pallor succeeded her blushes, caused by chagrin. She angrily stamped her foot and Lady Flayskin continued:

"You see for yourself your father approves of what I am doing. You... shall... be... whipped!" she concluded, accentuating every word.

"No! No! I will not!" cried the girl, struggling desperately to escape from the clutch of the two strong wenches.

But the latter did not allow themselves to be taken by surprise. They held Miss Virginia as in a vice. And in spite of her menaces and resistance they dragged her to the table and laid her upon it. They held her in position by her shoulders, while Mrs. Stuart and Mrs. Eagle tied a handkerchief round each wrist of the noble young lady. The handkerchiefs, drawn tight, were of great use in rendering the girl powerless.

Nevertheless, like a lioness caught in a snare, Miss Virginia continued her objurgations.

"Do not touch me! Take care not to be so foolhardy!"

The directress did not condescend to make reply again and occupied herself in raising the victim's petticoats. Miss Virginia kicked with such force that she would certainly have broken something had not Lady Flayskin, against whom the kicking was directed, been upon her guard.

The directress continued her occupation in an unconcerned manner. She raised the petticoats and fixed them by means of safety pins to the shoulders of the haughty young person. She gave terrible upheavals to the table and did her utmost to reach her enemy with her kicking feet.

In the meantime, adroit and astute Stella had not been idle. She had been in search of two straps with buckles, and she now held in her hands two long leather thongs such as are employed for doing up rolled travelling rugs. At a moment when Miss Virginia, lashing out like a mare, was again executing one of her vain efforts to kick the directress, ingenious and dextrous Stella caught a leg in one of her straps. As it terminated in a slip-knot, it was only necessary to give a pull in order to complete the abasement of the dignity of the young lady of noble descent, who fell forwards with her head on the table. Stella swiftly buckled the strap, which she had slipped down to the girl's ankle, to the leg of the table. It was then a very simple matter to get possession of the other ankle and quickly perform a like operation.

Lady Flayskin continued her preparations.

The young lady was now exposing to the view of the whole school the most lovely pair of legs imaginable. The calves were robust, showing a graceful line, while the ankles were of real distinction and the feet small and slender. Their possessor wore silk open-work stockings which allowed the pink skin to show through. Her little bronze buckled shoes were adorned with a large satin bow. Her position obliged her to thrust out her posterior and its curves were plainly revealed beneath the be-ribboned cambric drawers frilled with rich Irish point lace.

The directress vainly tried to make this garment slip down. She had to resort to the pair of scissors she always carried. It cut its way through obstructing bands and tapes until the garment slipped down between the young lady's legs, now rendered motionless.

What a superb hinder globe! How voluminous it was! The moon was not paler nor rounder. How majestic were its hemispheres in their amplitude and pearly pallor!

So august was the spectacle that this mocking assembly of scholars, accustomed to laugh at such sights, and throw ridicule on such nudity, held its breath. All the pupils, girls and boys alike, wept when it was their own turn to be flogged, and laughed when it was the turn of others, although their laughter as they watched a whipping was soon to be hysterical. But now, in presence of this aristocratic posterior, casting around its rays, so to speak, of pure glory, it was the muteness of adoration which reigned; religious silence compounded of pity and humble admiration.

In what condition were the onlookers destined soon to behold those imposing hindquarters when the ferocity of Lady Flayskin should have exercised itself on their incomparable charms?

The directress herself appeared not unmoved, but her emotion was of a curious and complex order. Her agitation comprised neither pity nor fear, qualities to which her heart had long been a stranger. Her hands, however, trembled slightly; her complexion usually so pale became ashy white, while lightning seem to shoot from beneath her half-closed eyelids. Doubtless she too was joining in the silent admiration in her own fashion, nevertheless not destined to prevent her laying a sacrilegious hand upon those splendours. Meanwhile, as she brandished the whip, her hand had almost a caressing air. It was with extraordinary gentleness, an infinity of precautions, and incomparable lightness of touch that she caused the drawers to slip down those legs so widely spread-eagled by astute Stella.

During this operation, the chemise for a moment fell forward, and was the cause of a transient eclipse of the white, nervous thighs and magnificent fleshy moon from which the class found it impossible to remove so much as an eyelid.

Lady Flayskin was in no hurry and after having slipped down the drawers in leisurely fashion, raised the chemise again with equal deliberation and fixed it by pins. as in the case of the petticoats, she attached the chemise to the girl's waist instead of to her shoulders. Her task completed. she drew back a step in the manner of an artist who has outlined his picture and wishes to try and imagine the effect when finished.

By the proud smile lighting up the face of the directress, it was understood that she was well satisfied with her progress up to the present.

The young victim was in an ideal posture for receiving a whipping of any imaginable nature. Each wrist firmly held by the handkerchiefs grasped by the two under-mistresses, her bosom extended upon the table; her feet fastened tightly to the table by strong straps; her back parts absolutely devoid of covering and thrust well out from the edge of the table, the young lady could present no obstacle nor resistance to the fury of the whip. The flogging was about to take its course.

The unfortunate victim maintained rigid silence although she felt herself to be now completely in the power of her enemy, a woman

who had never pardoned an affront and was not likely to do so to-
day for the first time.

Nevertheless, Miss Virginia appeared still unwilling to acknowledge the full gravity of her position although her case was now
desperate. Quite silent, she yet showed by her heavy breathing that
she continued to struggle with all the force of her muscles. The two
assistant mistresses had to support one another as they pulled upon
the handkerchiefs with all their strength in opposition to the violent
contractions of the body of the strong young lady. The trembling
movements of her thighs, the thrusting in and out of her posteriors
proved the victim's violent efforts to get her legs free, to release
herself from her bonds and have done with all restraint.

Lady Flayskin clearly perceived the meaning of the girl's efforts,
and also their futility. Far from being annoyed, she appeared to find
additional satisfaction in watching the struggles. For in truth she
judged that the flicker of hope still remaining in the girl's heart
would increase her victim's anguish and despair when the latter
found that after all she was completely powerless. The prolonging
of hope was the intensifying of subsequent suffering when the whip
in its fury should descend upon that living, still fighting flesh. And
in proportion as the courage slowly died, would the submission, the
abject subjection of spirit which should follow, be complete.

She was therefore far from being in a hurry. In the room reigned
heavy and expressive silence, broken only by the short sharp
breathing of the condemned girl, continuing her useless efforts. Nor
was there a pupil so bold as to dare to make a sound, so furious had
the directress's glance become.

At last Lady Flayskin judged the moment opportune to begin her
usual tirade.

"Miss Virginia, you have wearied the patience of your noble
father. After cruelly wounding the hearts of the devoted
governesses entrusted with your education, you have been judged
by the noble lord as incorrigible. No matter. You have been
entrusted by him to me and my task is now to reduce your
ungovernable disposition to docility. I have formally promised to be
successful and I would have you know that never have I failed to be
as good as my word. The promise I have given I regard as sacred. I

affirm to you in all solemnity that you shall not leave this room except in a tamed state, gentle as a lamb and more cringing than a dog. I am about to whip you without pity. In vain will you cry for mercy, in vain will you shriek for pity. I shall not cease to beat until my arms grow tired. I warn you that my arm is strong and that you will quickly perceive its prowess for yourself. My will is that when I have finished your flogging, you grovel at my feet, that is if you still have left strength enough to move. In my opinion, more probable is it that you will be carried from this room half dead, incapable of raising so much as a finger... Ah! you play at being proud! Do you feel the shame of having your posteriors exposed to view; your petticoats, raised above your head, and of being made the butt of all your schoolmates' mockery?"

At this point, the table gave a violent lurch, for Miss Virginia made a supreme effort to free herself. The two mistresses, however, were equal to their task and the leather straps resisted every strain. This wild and futile effort was the sole response given by Miss Virginia to the objurgations of the head-mistress. After a moment's pause, she continued:

"So you intend to remain silent? Very well. You shall make a full confession presently. Do your best to free yourself. Your struggles amuse me and your bonds are strong. You are unable to escape me and are absolutely in my power. I can do with you entirely as I choose, and it is my pleasure to make you remember this day so long as you live. I intend that never hereafter shall you think of this date of the year without a tremor. I am resolved that all your pride shall be uprooted by the whip. Not only shall I not spare you, but I shall crush you with an excess of severity. You shall scream aloud, implore for mercy, and address me in accents of agony faint and broken. You have refused to reply to my question. You are about to regret your mad obstinacy and pray for pardon with tears and cries. But I shall not pardon you. In the beating I shall give you, you will pay the total price of all your impertinence towards me. Between to-day and to-morrow, it is necessary for you to become the most docile pupil in my establishment."

At this moment, Miss Virginia struggled with such violence that the table was upset. The mistresses, however, had not relaxed their grip. They held on to the handkerchiefs in spite of finding themselves with their legs in the air and the edge of the table on top of them. Miss Virginia had found her feet, but was as helpless as ever, for she was unable to make the straps, which bound her ankles to the table's legs, give way, or to slip the said straps away from the table.

Even had she succeeded in freeing herself, she would probably have had full weight of the table upon her, with the weight of the two mistresses added thereto and would thus have been crushed. She was none the less highly elated by this partial victory and, ignorant of the nature of the bonds which hindered the movement of her legs, now exerted her whole strength to free herself further. The head-mistress on one side of her and Stella upon the other, managed to right the table, and this they did so speedily that a moment afterwards the young lady found herself roughly replaced in her original position. The two assistant mistresses fell back into a sitting posture, but still continued not to relax their hold upon the handkerchiefs which held the prisoner in place.

In this way, order was restored and Lady Flayskin determined to allow the victim time to meditate bitterly upon her disappointment.

"Don't lose heart! Add fresh faults to your old ones. I shall keep account of all. Had you resigned yourself to your fate, I might have lessened the severity of your punishment. Your obstinacy shows me that all compassion would be wasted and out of place. In order that repentance may sink deeply into your heart, it is necessary that the skin be entirely stripped from your posterior. Remain quiet and I will undertake to flog it perfectly. The whip will peel your skin off like a knife. It is my will that your blood flow in streams down your thighs to your heels. Hitherto your education has been conducted with gentleness. It is fitting that in this one day, all gentleness be banished therefrom."

The young girl kept her mouth firmly closed during this speech of Lady Flayskin, who was solemn and calm. She had decided to begin the actual flogging very shortly.

A whole minute; sixty livelong seconds had yet to pass, however, and meanwhile the whole class held their breath in suspense. These final preparations seemed to last a lifetime.

Lady Flayskin retired a step, and advanced again. Then, in order the better to measure her distance, she extended her arm. The quivering end of the heavy scourge of hide touched and seemed to tickle the spreading expanse of Miss Virginia's hinder charms. The young lady trembled at the outrage in a new fever of fury. This time the table did not move.

At last, the first blow fell!

Lady Flayskin had raised her arm on high and brought it down with a powerful sweep. Ghastly writhing was the sole response on the part of the victim, whose teeth were firmly set and who resolved to make not so much as a groan beneath the terrible whip. The pain, nevertheless, must have been indescribably acute, for the dull crash of the whip as it fell upon the living, writhing flesh made every ear tingle; while across the fine sphere so gloriously rounded, from one noble half to the other, stretched a livid weal which quickly turned to crimson.

Lady Flayskin had betrayed some anger on remarking that the blow had occasioned neither cries nor prayers for pity. Then she shrugged her shoulders. She knew well that the battle would end in her favour. No human courage could withstand the whip of hide. She began again.

A second blow was equally ineffectual in extorting so much as a groan from the courageous victim in spite of the torture she must have endured.

Was it possible that Lady Flayskin's cruelty was to be outdone by its victim's endurance?

By her expression of astonishment, the compression of her lips, the anger in her eyes, the onlookers for a moment were of that opinion.

Yet Lady Flayskin's long experience was of a nature to give her complete confidence in her powers. It appeared, moreover, to the pupils that in spite of the terrible nature of the blows she was not employing her full strength.

What then could be her project?

Why did she put a curb upon her terrible wrath?

The pupils were soon to know. They were to learn that by a refinement of cruelty, the moment of the first cry of pain was being delayed in order that when it should be wrung from the sufferer's throat, its agony should be far more intense and poignant.

In spite of this, no blow fell which did not leave its reddish-yellow weal, and already there was traced a network of livid lines. The first cut of all had now become a raised, horrible lump of flesh upon that unique and incomparable posterior, whose white purity had already been banished by the hail of stinging blows.

Suddenly, Lady Flayskin drew back a step and lowered the end of the stiff lash to the ground. Then, with a quick movement of her forearm she dealt a deadly blow from below, striking between the separated legs.

Immediately, a blood-curdling cry, inhuman in its agony, came from the tortured body of the victim.

This pitiless blow was succeeded by another of precisely the same nature on the same spot. Then the voice, hoarse with torture, of Miss Virginia was heard:

"Forgive me! Forgive me!"

"We will discuss the question of your forgiveness presently, Miss."

A third violent blow was directed at the delicate membrane.

"Oh! Stop! In the name of pity! Have done! I can't endure any more! Oh! I shall die of it! Have pity!"

"Did not I tell you so, Miss?"

"Oh! Have mercy!... Everything that you desire... I will do... My lady! My dear, good mistress; have pity upon me!"

"I have already told you, Miss, that I shall have no pity."

"Oh! You are killing me!"

"No. But I have not finished. The blood has not yet flowed, but this will make it!"

She had stepped to one side and raised herself on tiptoe. Then she lifted her whip on high and brought it down with a slashing blow across the buttocks.

The poor young lady gave a piercing cry, a yell of real agony.

"And here's another for the sake of variety!" said Lady Flayskin, striking a blow at right angles to the preceding one.

"Presently the marks will swell up. I shall then beat them. The skin will burst and the blood spurt out."

The girl was now in a pitiful condition. Beside herself with pain and terror, she uttered, in hoarse feeble tones, words without meaning, intermingled with faint cries and sobs.

The head-mistress addressed her.

"Well! Are you still as proud as before?"

"Oh! Oh! No!"

"I hope not indeed! Are you now disposed to obey me humbly and absolutely?"

"Oh! Oh! Oh! Yes!"

"I think so too. Nor do I think you will readily forget the respect you owe me. To make assurance doubly sure, here is something with which to engrave the memory of this duty upon your mind. As for me, I always keep my word. There is the noble red blood spouting from your behind. And I have not yet terminated..."

It was true. The flesh, which had swollen as the result of one of the first blows, had broken, and though the blood did not, as the directress averred, spout out, it nevertheless was oozing forth.

If it had been the design of the directress to increase her victim's terror by her highly coloured words, she fully succeeded.

It is probable that if at this particular moment, the two under-mistresses had not kept a very firm hold of the handkerchief which bound the victim's wrists, the poor girl would have fallen backwards, her body pulled over by the heavy weight of the hinder parts. She had fainted. The fact was established for certain when not so much as the slightest movement responded to the next blow. Not a groan was heard. It seemed the silence of death.

In such cases, the directress was wont to cease flogging immediately. Attentions of an energetic, if not very tender nature were lavished on the sufferer.

The present case offered no exception in this respect.

The two strong maid-servants, who shortly before had given such powerful aid in over coming the resistance of the young scholar, now re-entered the room. They had been dismissed so soon as the wrists of the victim had been firmly bound by the handkerchiefs of the under-mistresses, and in accordance with their instructions had waited outside the door until summoned to re-enter.

Lady Flayskin had used smelling-salts to the fainting girl, and poor Miss Virginia at length feebly opened her eyes. She looked around her in a dazed way and then wept showers of tears.

The two maids took hold of her, one under the armpits, the other by the feet, and in this way they carried her from the room. The scholars were conscious of an indescribable feeling of agitation although not a word was spoken. A feeling of terror and a deep stirring of the sensibilities were the chief effects of this scene upon those who witnessed it.

CHAPTER VI

For several days the girl was very ill. She lay upon her stomach in bed and cried out with terror so often as the maids pulled down the bedclothes with the charitable object of rubbing some oil into the skin of the injured parts.

I was well again before she was. It is true that my own whipping was mere child's play in comparison with that to which the cruelty of the head-mistress had treated her, with the object of crushing her haughty disposition once for all.

When she returned to her lessons, therefore, I was able to witness the effects produced.

Ah, what gentleness of expression! What humility of mien! Strange indeed was the contrast between this timorous self-effacement and those haughty airs we had witnessed when first she came among us! She now seemed fearful of exciting the least attention. Directly the head-mistress entered the class-room, every eye was turned upon Miss Virginia. The girl dropped her head upon her bosom; her face was strangely pale and she trembled like a leaf.

Lady Flayskin signed to her to follow her. Miss Malville obeyed instantly.

After her interview with the head-mistress, she was even paler than when she rose to leave the room, while she appeared to have difficulty in making the least movement. Her waist had become smaller and it was plain that she wore a corset very tightly laced. Her elegant buckled shoes she wore no longer, but, instead, high boots with high heels of an exaggerated type, excessively arched at the instep.

We were not long in learning what had transpired. For, in this establishment, the servants were as communicative as we were inquisitive. The head-mistress was alone in the belief that anything was kept really concealed in this extraordinary school.

When Miss Virginia, in obedience to the imperious gesture, had followed the head-mistress into the latter's private room, she did so as though hypnotised. Her walk was halting, plainly showing that her legs tottering beneath her, could scarcely support her body.

When the door closed behind her in the private room of Lady Flayskin, the girl in an apparently overpowering access of devotion, seized the hem of the mistress's robe and put it fervently to her lips. The mistress removed her dress from the girl's hands, and said to her gently, as slavishly she knelt before her:

"Do not fall from one excess into another. Too proud to begin with, you are now too humble. Get up, sit there, and listen attentively to what I have to say to you."

The girl, slightly confused, sat down on the edge of a chair. Her pose expressed extreme contrition.

"This is what I have to say to you, Miss Malville. Greatly to my personal regret, I have been obliged to employ the whip in order to tame you. I hope and believe that the lesson will not be without its fruit. You will not oblige me to subject you to so terrible a chastisement..."

At this point, Lady Flayskin's words were broken into by a storm of tears and sobs. Miss Virginia's whole frame quivered with anguish and uncontrollable emotion as she recalled what she had been through. In tones of entreaty, she cried:

"Oh! Never! Ah! My lady, it was indeed awful!"

"Did you deserve your punishment!"

"Yes, my lady!" said the poor girl with lowered eyes, deep crimson suffusing the cheeks so deathly pale a moment before.

"It is an excellent practice to confess the faults we have committed."

She looked fixedly at the girl and continued:

"Pay good heed to what I say. When you arrived here and your father, worthy Lord Malville, presented you to me, I was able to sum you up in a moment. Virginia, you have excellent qualities, but unfortunately the deplorable education to which you were subjected before entering these walls had stifled those qualities. It was clear to me, from the moment my eyes first rested on you, that I should have to commence by seriously flogging you. That first step has been made. I have now no anxiety as to your tractability."

Here the girl burst anew into tears and sobs, replying to this diagnosis of her case:

"Yes, indeed, my lady!"

The mistress motioned to her to be silent and said severely:

"I will add that you have further to learn not to interrupt. In a young girl, no conduct could appear more bold and disgracious. Apply yourself to the task of learning to listen to the end, irrespectively of the nature of the words addressed to you."

After a moment's pause to assure herself that her words had gone home, she continued:

"I have therefore had preliminary recourse to the whip because otherwise I should have failed in exacting that absolute deference to my every wish which I require in the case of all my pupils. A moment ago, I spoke of your remarkable natural qualities. You are very intelligent. I am sure of it. The difficulty has been that your instructors have been ignorant, that is all. Again, your physical charms are of high order, for you are beautiful, Virginia. Your beauty, however, has been neglected."

She had drawn her chair close up to that of the girl and, stooping down, now took one of the latter's feet into her hands. Contemptuously she drew off one low shoe and her fingers moved lightly and caressingly across the open-work silk stocking on the sole of the foot.

The girl gave a nervous laugh and cried:

"Oh! my lady, stop! You tickle me!"

The mistress appeared not to hear and continued this strange treatment of a pupil by first lightly touching the ankle with her active fingers and then pushing her hand up the leg until it rested upon the firm-fleshed, well rounded calf.

"Shoes! What an idea to wear shoes like a waiting-woman when this strong and graceful leg would show to such good effect in a high boot! You require a narrow long boot of fine kid, with polished tips, and heels so high that you would appear three inches taller than you are. You must have an arched boot that shall do justice to your charming instep. Yes, certainly! Presently you shall put on the boots you see here. They have been made expressly for you, to your measure; but the makers have been instructed to design them narrower than your shoes which they have had as a pattern. Your old shoes must be quite shabby from use."

"Oh, not in the least, my lady!"

"I have already told you that you are not to interrupt me. It is even more important that you do not contradict me."

"Certainly, my lady. What are you doing? Oh! I beg you to leave me alone! Oh! do stop!"

Lady Flayskin was fingering the drawers above the thighs and she said in accents of scorn:

"I have never heard of such an idea! What a corset! And as for this busk it has no rigidity whatever. It is soft, it is yielding and useless. The bones of a corset must be hard and unyielding."

Her fingers continued groping, while Miss Virginia, with head thrown back, laughed hysterically.

Lady Flayskin at length ceased her researches and said:

"You must at once remove all this trumpery and put on the clothes which you see here. You must have remarked that we have a school uniform. We are all of us devotees of Saint Muslin. Muslin is cool, becoming, and in every way suitable for young girls. Your silk dress, on the contrary, is exceedingly pretentious. I repeat that you must try and get accustomed to our modesty of bearing. Modesty is the noblest ornament a woman can wear and that which man prizes, when he discovers it, more than all our other charms. It is therefore essential that your under garments should be selected with great care. What is more captivating than a slender waist? It is our waist that gives us that gracefulness and lightness of carriage which distinguishes us from men, and it is a tight-laced corset alone which gives us this distinguishing feature. In short, it is the corset which marks the woman of superior civilisation from her humbler sisters. Without it, a woman may possess good looks, but she will remain heavy, massive, almost animal. The corset is the bestower not only of beauty and elegance but also of poise. Where the wearer has already grace of bearing, her grace will be accentuated; should she be ungraceful, it is the corset which will give her the charm she lacked, on condition that the lacing is tightly drawn. What can you hope for from an appliance such as you have upon you at this moment? Those ridiculous whalebones with no resistance, are no support whatever. See, too, how easily I bend them and how simple a matter it is to pass my fingers beneath your corset. Why, dear Virginia, you are not drawn in the least! We must immediately remedy matters."

She had been suiting the action to her words and her fingers which she had slipped beneath the corset were tickling the hips of the girl who twisted herself about and laughed without pleasure.

"Undress yourself, Virginia, that I may see you in all the glory of your beauty."

Had such an order been given to the haughty girl a few days previously, that is to say, before the memorable flogging, she would only, in reply, have laughed disdainfully and sardonically.

Undress herself?

It was the lady's maid upon whom that duty devolved. Of what use is it to be the daughter of a noble house, if one is not to have servants at one's beck and call? And if the lady's maid cannot come immediately, some other woman of the household must do the bidding of her young mistress.

Doubtless such would have been the thoughts passing though Miss Virginia's brain a few days before and she would not have failed to communicate them to lady Flayskin, who in the opinion of the young lady — which she would not have hesitated to communicate — could and ought to serve her pupil as lady's maid. Was she not Miss Virginia Malville, a member of a family far more ancient and powerful than that to which Lady Flayskin belonged?

At the present moment any feeling of repugnance at the notion of baring her body before anyone except a serving-woman, did not cross the mind of the haughty young lady.

Very obediently, she sat down and, to begin with, drew off the shoe which the mistress had not removed. She then unhooked her dress, and unconsciously returning to her manner of former days cast the garment aside, negligently careless as to how or where it fell.

The directress immediately scolded her with severity.

"Among the principal of feminine qualities is that of order. The future of a girl who lacks this sovereign quality offers no assurance, and her riches will avail her nothing. Man is well aware of the value of this quality and should he find himself united to an untidy, wasteful woman, he is not slow to make his partner's life a burden to her. Take up the dress you have so carelessly cast into that corner! Fold it carefully and hang it over the back of this chair. Do you understand me?"

The girl replied confusedly in a low tone:

"Yes, my lady."

She took off her petticoat and her corset, the latter with perfect ease, then her drawers of fine cambric, embroidered with satin. The drawers slipped down her thighs, seemed to catch for a moment at the calves of the legs, and finally lay round the little feet. The girl looked at the garment hesitatingly and Lady Flayskin kindly remarked:

"I understand your hesitation. For a young girl, it is disagreeable to have to rid her legs of her drawers in the presence of another person. This notion, however, must be overcome, for it is only a notion. Come, courage, my dear pupil!"

The girl appeared electrified by these words, affectionate though they were, and drew her legs resolutely free from her drawers and petticoat. Then, as in the case of the other garments, she hung these also over a chair, observing scrupulous care to do so in an orderly way, for she had not forgotten the ominous words Lady Flayskin addressed to her after her previous negligence.

Her chemise now only remained and a thin silk vest which the girl wore next her skin. The chemise was only held for a moment by the ample hips before it slipped down. Lady Flayskin, in her impatience, was acting as lady's maid, quite forgetful of her dignity. Her ready hands aided the descent of the chemise and then grasped the narrow sleeve of the vest. The girl was thus able to rid herself of both garments the more speedily.

Then the mistress, her eyes glistening with pleasure, surveyed her patrician pupil.

It would not have been possible to find a statue whose beauty was at once so correct, classic, and at the same time so attractive, graceful, and harmonious. Supple and vigorous force was betrayed in every movement of the slender frame.

The girl's colour was pink and white. Her skin was incomparably smooth and transparent. It was the true British complexion, the tint of a delicate English rose.

Her hair was a wealth of gleaming burnished gold. Its Venetian tint is even rarer on the shore of the Adriatic than amid the fogs of London. Her mouth was small, beautifully chiselled, and of a deep cherry-red. Her eyes were of a colour impossible to define, for it changed with every angle and degree of light. Sometimes they were grey as the sea beneath a cloudy wind-swept sky.

A moment afterwards, they would reflect the darkness of unfathomable watery depths.

But if her complexion was exquisite, what words shall describe her grace of symmetry?

Miss Virginia's body was at the same time elegant and charming and of the purest classicism. Her flesh was neither too abundant nor insufficient. In her proud young purity, she held her graceful head erect and the points of her firm breasts were turned skywards like wild strawberries on a bed of snow. Her neck was swan-like, and her arms would have matched those of a Spartan wrestling woman as revealed to us by the sculptors of Greece. Her legs were the noble limbs of Diana.

In short, the girl's aristocratic beauty was that of the three goddesses who upon Ida's Mount disputed the vote of the shepherd and competed for the apple of discord. Miss Virginia's beauty was as moving and seductive as that of Venus and as unapproachable as that of Juno, while to her other charms seemed to be added something of the calm and repose of wise Minerva.

I employ these high-sounding terms because I am reporting the head-mistress's own eulogy of her pupil.

Lady Flayskin, during her careful examination of Miss Virginia, made use of all these expressions and of many others also which I shall not repeat. Her feelings became too much for her and in the exceedingly descriptive and familiar language in which she dwelt upon some of those charms of her pupil which are not usually alluded to, she forgot her usual hypocrisy.

Miss Virginia could only deeply blush, thus adding new charm to her beauty. She scarcely moved, except to show the lines of her figure to better effect, her long hair descending in a stream of glory almost to her little pink heels.

The mistress placed a hand affectionately upon the firm rounded haunches of her pupil and said:

"The marks do not show any more. It was far from my intention to spoil so incomparable a masterpiece. Now had I with this rough and heavy lash struck with all my strength, red scars would now mark this adorable flesh; frightful marks disfiguring your lily skin. I am content, quite content... Ah! Virginia, I wish you to be with me the happiest of girls. I wish to bring you to that perfection of which the Bible speaks... Yes, I wish..."

While speaking, she put her arms around the big, bare, supple body, and pressing her lips to those of her pupil, fanned her with burning breath.

Then she drew her towards a large sofa in order to talk more comfortably.

Lady Flayskin took off her own clothes also and remarked:

"You see I am not without beauty even as compared with you."

Never had the head-mistress shown herself so affectionate with any of her pupils.

If she was wont to give free course to her vice, if she did not oppose the slightest check upon her passionate desires, she nevertheless managed to do all with absolute self-control, both as regards actions and words. She would proceed to the worst Lesbian extremities while talking of the lofty claims of morality. Her victims did not know in the least what to think. Sometimes the girls would be convinced that Lady Flayskin, who had just made some most moral discourse, must be a saint; while an hour afterwards her actions would render them as perplexed as ever.

In the present instance, Miss Virginia's physical feelings, under the treatment of the skilled and passionate mistress, became of a kind she had never previously experienced. Unconsciously she returned the burning kisses she was receiving.

Both mistress and pupil became possessed with extraordinary sensual exaltation. In the case of Virginia, little or no attempt was made to control the tide of delirious, delicious sensations. Each would cast herself into the arms of the other and then for a moment they would slowly draw apart and look with glowing burning eyes at the spectacle of unveiled beauty before them. Then with the tips of their fingers they would lightly touch one another and kiss until almost frenzied with delight.

The mistress was the first to recover herself. In slow and measured tones, after her usual manner, she made the following hypocritical speech:

"Beauty, Miss, is not the only requisite. You cannot appear as you are usually dressed in a drawing-room. In our country, the first country of the world, we are not excessively prudish. In Society, low-necked dresses are more than tolerated. A young girl, no matter how pure and stainless she may be, is permitted to show nearly the whole of her bust. But this she must do with skill and as though seeking to conceal what a thin gauze covering reveals only too intoxicatingly to her dazzled partner in the waltz. His feelings are deeply stirred as there rises to his enraptured senses the fragrance of the breasts, this centre of feminine seduction. The arms may also be exposed. In my opinion, however, their allurement is considerably enhanced when concealed by long close-fitting gloves of a dark tint. A little bare skin above the elbow, but only a little, should be shown. This partial exposure will be found sufficient to conquer admirers.

"If I frequently insist upon the importance of such matters, it is because the duty of a woman consists, if she would assure herself of happiness, in her ability to attach indissolubly the desires of men to her charms. Men have predominance over women as regards muscular or brute force, but we, with our powers of seduction, are able to crush their boasted strength to a pulp. Let us learn therefore to use our gifts nobly and well. You, dear Virginia, are of a becoming height. If the high heels which I oblige you to wear were designed solely for accentuating the height, in your case at any rate, they would be of no advantage. But they serve ultimately to give to the deportment charming seriousness and well-bred dignity, fitting in well with that timidity of character which, in the eyes of the stronger sex, is not the least of our attractions. By curious contradiction, the style of deportment to which I allude, gives us at the same time a certain boldness of appearance which is a useful corrective to an air of timidity possibly so pronounced as to inspire masculine admirers with fear to approach and disturb such coy and shrinking charms. The boot which reaches high up the leg conveys the impression of beauty of a proud imperious order, made for the crushing of hearts beneath our feet; and, at the same time, such a boot is symbolical of the slavery to which, of one's own will or through the energy of a man, we are momentarily subjected. Need I remark to you that your narrow, high-bred foot would profit by being adorned with a long tight boot? Your instep is already finely arched, but its line would gain in grace through the wearing of an exceedingly arched boot with heels so high that the toes should be almost vertically beneath the level of the heel? See, too, how these heels are scooped out. Dubarry herself wore nothing more skilfully designed. These boots, intended for your use, are, you must acknowledge, veritable jewels or, to describe them better, perfect caskets suited for the treasures they will enclose. Here, dear Miss Malville, are your stockings. Your usual ones are pretty, but you must observe the rules of my academy. Naturally, I have chosen excellent silk, in preference to any material of less value. See how soft they are! Put them on carefully, drawing them up properly, for one of the rules of this establishment is that stockings shall never show a wrinkle."

The girl crossed one leg over the other, as she sat on the edge of the couch, and obediently began to put on a stocking. Lady Flayskin watched her with a look of graciousness and amusement, for truly, the homely position gave the girl additional attractiveness. The variety of her charms was not indeed Virginia's least attraction. She put on both stockings with the carefulness, as regarded creases, to which she had been enjoined, and then received the boots from her mistress's hands.

But now her task was not so simple. The mistress had characterised the little low shoes which Virginia was in the habit of wearing as flabby and shabby. They fitted her exactly with no room to spare. Lady Flayskin had, consequently, given instructions to the boot maker to make the footgear much narrower than the pattern entrusted to him. Poor Virginia had therefore now to wrestle with an insoluble problem, the insertion in a given space of a body greater than that space. But woman boldly faces what to the logician appears impossible, and she conquers. Virginia made many wry but becoming grimaces, heaved some big sighs, uttered sundry little cries, appeared greatly at a loss, even shed some tears, and finally struck forcibly on the ground with her heel, like an impatient mare pawing the soil, and finally succeeded in finding one foot within a boot. She paused a moment for breath. Then she resolutely set about getting the other boot on, while also declaring that she was horribly pinched and that never would she be able to walk in boots so narrow and uncomfortable.

Lady Flayskin corrected her in tones of severity.

"You must learn that it is necessary to be able to suffer in order to be beautiful. These boots fit you perfectly. See how wonderfully well your foot is now set off and how the calf now shows to advantage. Presently, when you have buttoned both boots up, you will speak differently. You will thank me. The slight feeling of pain will, it is true, moderate your gratitude, but that feeling will pass as the leather yields and your feet grow used to their new covering. You will then be proud to be so well shod, for, I repeat, we are now dealing with a point of prime importance in your apparel."

The pretty pupil had succeeded in getting both boots on, and standing by the sofa, she placed alternatively one foot and then the other thereon in order to fasten the buttons. Such irreverent treatment of her sofa, Lady Flayskin would not have tolerated in the case of any other pupil.

Virginia was clothed only in her creaseless black silk stockings and her high boots, the latter reflecting the light from their polished tips. Her large posterior was thrust far out, as she bent to her task, showing her back, narrow at the waist and broadening at the shoulders. The girl appeared superb in this attitude.

It was consequently not without a little sigh of regret that Lady Flayskin painted out to her the chemise of fine lawn together with the other garments intended for her use, all of which were laid out on a chair near her.

As the dressing began, the mistress sighed anew as she watched the partial eclipse of the perfect breasts, the snowy thighs and the peerless hinder globes.

Nevertheless, Miss Virginia's chemise did not by any means annihilate her seductiveness. Her aristocratic pride was now tempered by the modesty she had had instilled into her by the whip. She was moreover a spotless virgin. The net result was an inexpressible charm, greatly to the taste of the perverse-minded directress of the establishment who was a veritable *connaisseuse* in sensual impressions, from long experience.

After another interval of silent admiration, Lady Flayskin said:

"Now see how well your clothes become you! Admire once more the boots which fit you to perfection. It is difficult for you to believe how they will enhance your attractiveness. Drawers and chemise are necessary parts of a lady's costume, but there is a garment of more importance. I place the boots, important though they are, below the stays, and please do not interpret this words in any ridiculous fashion. As regards any such interpretation, I have something to say to you. You have just smiled during my address to you. Accustom yourself to listen to everything I say to you, not only without interrupting, but without giving any sign either of approval or of disapproval. In a word, do not show any feeling whatever. The only requisite, which politeness renders obligatory, is profound attention. Do not forget."

"No, my lady."

"Do you understand the importance of my words?"

"Perfectly, my lady."

"I congratulate you. I am decidedly of opinion that the whip has been most profitable to you. Are you not of the same opinion?"

"Certainly, my lady."

"Nevertheless, I shall not be so exacting as to expect you to thank me for your whipping. That, probably, you would find it difficult to do with any heartiness. Am I not correct in my surmise?"

Both laughed, Lady Flayskin with open amusement, Miss Malville in a constrained and rather frightened way. It was a desire to please which had made her laugh, for she was afraid.

Poor girl, she had been right in her fears! Her astute mistress had had her own reasons for recalling to the mind of the pupil the cruel flogging with the thong of hide.

Her object was simply to make the girl comprehend perfectly, in the case of the smallest notion of rebellion remaining in the latter's mind, that it was indispensable for her to submit to the disciplining power of the corset unless she desired a second application of the treatment which had reduced her posteriors to such a sorry state.

Miss Malville quite understood the mistress's meaning and her terror of the corset was not diminished on that account.

The reality far surpassed her expectations. The pair of stays had evidently been made by a corset-maker of the highest class. Both shape and material showed it to be the work of an artist. That was indisputable. The other pupils had to be content with corsets of strong linen, but this was of brocaded silk and the workmanship had been carefully and beautifully finished off. The whalebone and steel stiffeners were numerous and seemed at first to be of an extreme rigidity. Such, however, was not the case. This corset, in its pronounced and fashionable model, was as supple as it was elegant.

Miss Malville, on holding it in her hands, was not at first disposed to greatly fear it. But so soon as she had it on her body and endeavoured to hook it, her difficulties began. The more the girl tried to perform her task, the more hopelessly impossible that feat appeared.

Her ladyship watched these unsuccessful efforts with an interested and ill-boding eye. She did not yet, however, intervene.

Miss Malville drew her stomach in, raised her arms high, exhausted herself, stopped, recommenced her impossible task, but all to no purpose. She was then about to loosen the side-lacing and thus make the stays larger.

"Ah! I emphatically forbid you to do that!" exclaimed Lady Flayskin. "Then how shall I manage?"

"Set to work honestly, with courage, and without being afraid of pinching your skin. What? You do not know how to put on a corset?"

"But this corset is not like others!"

"It is you who are not like others!"

Virginia lowered her head, raised it anew, and struggled with might and main, but all to no purpose.

Her ladyship's tone became menacing.

"I am afraid there is trouble in store!"

But Virginia replied, in a somewhat sulky tone:

"It is impossible!"

She held the corset in her hands, uncertain as to what she was to do with it.

Lady Flayskin took a chair in front of her and looking at her fixedly, said, with lips trembling with anger:

"You are going to put it on immediately."

The young girl, overcome by her hard and useless struggle, burst into tears and sobs.

"I cannot! I cannot!"

"Yes, you can!"

"I tell you that I cannot!"

"Say that you will not!"

"Oh!"

"Oh's" and "ah's" are useless. I give you two minutes in which to put it on and fasten it."

With a significant air, the mistress went to the drawer of the large cupboard where the birches were ranged in order. She searched among them, making a whistling sound with the twigs similar to that made by the autumnal leaves which whirl together as they fall. Poor Virginia could not help being moved by this sinister noise. Her teeth chattered and, in consequence she bit her tongue. This little accident is often very painful and, in this case, Virginia in her momentary suffering, opened her hands and dropped the corset to the ground.

Terrified by the probable consequences of this fresh misfortune, the poor girl now sank upon a chair, covered her face with her hands and wept bitterly.

To add to her affliction, the wrathful mistress had at length fixed upon her selection of a rod. The chosen instrument was long and thin, and its tapering proportions were such as to inspire the greatest terror as it cut through the air — the directress was already swishing it hither and thither in a horrible manner.

Virginia's sobs redoubled, but she showed no signs of an intention to renew her efforts with the corset.

Her ladyship addressed her:

"Well! I am waiting for you."

The girl was stung by the injustice and cried:

"It is impossible, as you very well know."

Lady Flayskin adopted a more conciliatory tone and said:

"Shall we try together?"

"It is useless. The stays are too small!"

"Mind what you are saying!"

"Oh! If you were to whip me to death, you would not succeed in getting this corset fastened."

"We shall see. I have offered you my aid, a thing I never do, and you have refused it. I shall help you, nevertheless, but not until after I have first well whipped you. It is fitting that you should experience the difference between the birch-rod and the cane. The latter is, it is true, an instrument of greater ferocity than the birch, but the rod has a treacherous cunning all its own."

"Leave me alone! Leave me alone! I don't want to be whipped. I prefer to but on the corset."

"You shall first be whipped. Certainly you shall put on this corset and I will help you. But since you have defied me to whip you to death, I accept your challenge. I am not in the habit of taking no notice of such high speeches. Once again you have been impertinent in spite of my kindness and it is necessary to punish you. Come, go down on your knees in front of the sofa. Put your face on the edge. Like that! Yes! Draw up your chemise and hold it in your hands. Take care not to let it fall again nor to try to protect your posteriors with your hands."

The girl was now indeed and object for pity as she cried for mercy with tears and entreaties. But she obeyed without delay the bidding of the mistress, who was secretly delighted with this tractableness and docility. Henceforward, plainly, the once high-spirited, haughty girl would show herself completely tamed and cowed by the whip, ready in every particular to render complete obedience to her mistress now and to her master later on.

Virginia awaited her punishment kneeling humbly, ready to endure upon her protruding posterior the penalty which a fault of so slight and venial a nature had incurred.

The mistress stepped forward with heart untouched by the charms before her. It seemed rather that her wrath was stimulated by the sight of this vast globe which reflected so little of the emotions of the unfortunate young lady. Lady Flayskin felt that these spheres were mocking her as she laid a preliminary cut across them causing an electric tremor, as it were, to stir their phlegmatic placidity.

Then, in no way disarmed by the tears, cries, protestations and groans of the girl, Lady Flayskin whipped her with her usual power and assurance, yet calmly and methodically as was fitting in a lady of her position. She did not neglect, however, to put all her strength into her task.

She could allow herself to go to work with the utmost energy without running any risk of injuring the beautiful hinder part whose correction she had undertaken. She had selected the longest and most slender of the birches. The one she was now employing consisted of six birch-tree twigs tied together. They were of extraordinary elasticity, strength and length, and the rod was a real work of art in which the maker, Lady Flayskin, had displayed consummate skill.

There could be no doubt that the rod was an ideal one, admirably adapted for inflicting a thousand cruel smarts upon the skin's surface, together with the most painful yearnings. It was an instrument for drawing the blood up to the rounded surface, but not for making it flow. Rather was it a meet revel for the outpouring of passion, for firing a soul with ardour unquenchable. This whip's true end was not the infliction of cruel punishment. It was an instrument for breaking the skin without causing blood to appear. It was a whip for amorous cruelty, one such as the tenderest of lovers would wish to possess wherewith to soften the heart of his mistress by a sting and a caress. It was at the same time designed rather to inspire love than fear.

Yet as this rod sang and whistled in the air and descended whack! on the tender surface of a sensitive part of the young lady, the globe could not but writhe its vast proportions in a fashion which the malicious flogger found extremely tasteful.

The pearl-like skin assumed the appearance of marble veined

with purple and rose-red streaks. The magnificent crupper, so impertinent a short time previously, seemed now to blush with confusion.

The poor girl cried out that she was being done to death and that she intended to offer no resistance to her murderer, that her sufferings were unspeakable. These cries were broken by groans of agony, but nothing availed to arouse the compassion of her ladyship who well knew what she was about.

She found her employment too enjoyable to abandon it yet awhile.

She seemed indeed to devote herself to her task with ever increasing gusto, and without for a moment forgetting the particular methods of applying the rod which a long experience had shown to be most efficacious. She had stood first on the right side and had flogged the hemispheres crosswise. Now she stood on the left side and performed the same process.

Then she had taken a curious implement and put it within reach of her and before employing it.

It consisted of an ebony stick of about a foot in length. At each extremity, was a widely branching fork to which was attached a strap and buckle. This she inserted between the legs of the poor girl who could see nothing of these sinister preparations, but who trembled the more for her uncertainty.

She did well to tremble.

Lady Flayskin attached the straps to the victim's knees. Virginia was now obliged by the ebony rod to keep her legs apart, nor could she possibly rise to her feet.

The preparations finished, her ladyship placed herself behind the girl and laid a firm hand on her neck. Pitilessly deaf to the piercing shrieks of the unfortunate victim, and easily controlling all efforts to escape her hold, she proceeded with all her strength to flog lengthwise, from below upwards.

The rod whistled and curled and the girl writhed and squirmed beneath this cruelty.

It was no use for her to cry in broken syllables that she would prefer, ten times over, the hide-covered scourge; that her sufferings were more than she could bear. It was in vain that she entreated her pitiless mistress to finish with one good bow rather than kill her by inches. In spite of all she could cry or entreat, she was destined to drink her cup of agony to the dregs — or, at any rate, until the arm of Lady Flayskin grew tired.

The flogging was plainly of long duration, and Virginia was more dead than alive when at length she was freed from the curious thigh-dividing implement which had exposed her tenderest parts to the biting cruelty of the birch without enabling her to protect herself in the least from its stinging attacks.

With maternal solicitude, her ladyship now took the weeping girl and raising her in her arms, laid her upon the sofa where she continued to sob, her face covered by her arm, in a manner to touch the most unfeeling heart.

Was savage Lady Flayskin touched? In any case, it is a matter of knowledge that she took a bottle of very old sherry, uncorked it with the respect its venerable antiquity merited and filled two glasses with the really precious wine. One she placed for herself, while the other she offered to her weeping, but still beautiful pupil.

She said to her quite simply:

"Your very good health?"

The girl had withdrawn the arm which covered her face and she now looked with an air of stupefaction at this glass of fine crystal reflecting the warm rich colouring of the topaz hued liquid. What the liquid might be, Virginia did not know, but she looked with dark suspicion, as was natural, at every gesture of Lady Flayskin.

In bitter tones she demanded:

"Is this the consummation of your treatment of me? Do you think now to poison me?"

With a smile of indulgent pity for such folly, the directress, for all reply, put to her own lips the glass she had poured out for herself, drank it off and smacked her lips with an air of enjoyment.

The girl became ashamed of her ridiculous suspicion, did what she had seen done, and found herself feeling much better in consequence. She felt new strength in her body; the sense of prostration caused by the whipping seemed to disappear as the generous wine warmed her blood.

She felt indeed as though she were being warmed by a veritable flame which coursed through her veins increasing the great vibration of the nerves caused by the skilful flogging of Lady Flayskin.

Seeing her rosy cheeks and bright eyes, where tears, which only a moment before had ceased to flow, shone like dewdrops and more brightly than diamonds, Lady Flayskin could not help being moved. Such sweetness and charm compelled her to imprint a kiss upon the cherry lips which immediately returned the token with interest. Yet again was prolonged intercourse exchanged between the woman and the lass upon the sofa and in an exceedingly agreeable fashion.

The directress, however, returned obstinately to her original purpose.

"Now, dearest, we are going to use our united efforts with the corset."

The girl, overwhelmed with grief, entreated.

"Spare me the suffering, I beg you!"

"Little fool! It is for your good."

"My good, my happiness is to be like this near you, in comfort, free to move about. It is infinite delight. You are wicked! wicked! Let me kiss your beautiful hand at once so cruel and so kind."

"Child!" gasped the mistress.

"Your child! Will you permit it? You shall be my loved mother. But, I beg you, never whip me again as you have to-day."

"You are going to be whipped immediately and in the same manner unless you get up and take your stays."

"Oh!"

With a bound, the girl was on her feet. She rushed to the corset and with lips compressed, stomach thrust in, holding her breath the while, began her vain contortions of a short time previously. Now she was to be aided by the mistress. The latter came behind her and placed her knee against the large stern of her pupil. At the same time with both her hands, she thrust forward the two sides of the stays, causing the corset to gradually make its way over the hips.

At one moment, Miss Malville thought the task was accomplished, and in her satisfaction, she permitted herself to take a long breath, an action she had tried for some moments not to indulge in.

Everything had to be begun again.

Lady Flayskin, who had felt her fingers forced back by the irresistible force of the girl's expanding sides as she took breath, became enraged and hissed:

"Well! What are you doing, little fool?"

"The most natural thing, my lady, I am breathing."

"Know then that I am in no mood for joking! A jest should never be made when a task is in course of accomplishment."

The pretty pupil laid the words to heart. The fruitless efforts recommenced. At a moment when the stud seemed on the point of being caught properly by the hook, Miss Virginia, with a piercing cry, loosed her hold. She had inadvertently, though excusably, in her state of mind, caught a little of her delicate skin under the hook and the pain had caused her to loose hold of both hook and stud.

At length, however, one hook was fast. It was then that Miss Virginia shrieked in agony, declaring that her ladyship, while helping her, was hurting her cruelly by pinching her flesh.

Lady Flayskin consented to a moment of respite, only to inquire if her pupil would prefer to continue the task under the whip? Such a suggestion on the part of her implacable mistress did not fail to terrify the young girl.

She did her utmost to make her efforts match those of the more skilful Lady Flayskin whose fingers were engaged in pulling and working the material which seemed as though it would never yield to any treatment. Her ladyship, however, worked with confidence and without pity for the unfortunate girl's flesh, which frequently became caught under the hooks, and poor Virginia who scarcely dared to breathe, had naturally no intention of groaning.

In this way the work went on for an hour, counting the time involved in necessary moments of rest, and then, quite suddenly as frequently happens in such cases, the hooks seemed to close over the buttons as by a miracle.

Her ladyship was as supremely content as if she had concluded the finest of masterpieces, and inquired:

"Well?"

Silence was the sole response.

But the expression on the pale face of the poor girl, the terrible dilatation of her large eyes, the half opened mouth from which her breath seemed to hiss out like gas escaping, all this made up a reply which, for all its silence, was none the less eloquent.

The heart of Lady Flayskin remained adamantine and she remarked:

"You see now! You have done your task and it was easy enough. But I notice that the stays fit too loosely; they are not drawn in at all. Come here and let me arrange that for you."

The poor girl, with the stiff steps of an automaton, approached the mistress. She might have been a German soldier, as without turning her head to either right or left by so much as a quarter of an inch, and without bending a knee, she made her military advance. By the way in which she put her foot to the ground and the wry face which accompanied the movement, it was plain that she suffered from her narrow new boots with their exaggerated high heels and endless high sheaths which so pinched and compressed both leg and ankle. The sufferings from the boots were very real, but they did not count, so to speak, in comparison with the agonies she was now enduring from the corset.

She stopped before the mistress with a precision in her right-about half-turn which a soldier of his Imperial Majesty the German Emperor might have envied. Lady Flayskin put a knee against the magnificent posterior and, taking hold of the laces, pulled with all her strength.

She then said that her efforts were being opposed by the girl whose sides were expanding spasmodically though for a most natural reason. The lungs by a reflex movement were struggling for their existence. The instinct of self-preservation is stronger than an intention to be obedient; stronger too than fear of the whip, and the girl was powerless in the grip of that instinct.

With an unpleasant laugh, the head-mistress pushed her victim towards an angle of the room across which was placed a small cupboard. Lady Flayskin was never at a loss for expedients. When she had an end in view no difficulty was permitted to oppose her for long. She had an expedient for surmounting every obstacle in her path. Virginia obeyed the push given her as though she had been a moving corpse.

The little cupboard, when opened, was found to contain, screwed down upon a stand, a pretty little capstan, similar in all respects to those employed on ships for raising the anchor. A strong silk cord was wound round it, ending in a steel hook. The handles for turning the miniature capstan were wanting, for they were, in fact, unnecessary. Lady Flayskin attached the lace of the corset to the steel hook and then pressed an electric button. The capstan then proceeded to turn with extreme deliberation while the unfortunate victim cried in scarcely audible tones that she could feel her bones cracking in her chest.

The capstan continued to turn.

Virginia, with a desperate gesture, raised her hands to her throat, crying:

"I am on fire! Air! I stifle!"

The capstan still turned, but with such slowness that a single revolution had not yet been completed.

The girl beat the air with her arms. She opened her mouth, but no sound now did she make. Her eyes rolled convulsively. A small spot of blood appeared at the corner of the mouth. She fell forwards and her face must have struck the ground had she not been held up by the hook.

Immediately the finger of Lady Flayskin was raised from the electric button and the capstan ceased to revolve.

Virginia, in a dead faint, head hanging forwards, hands touching the ground, feet resting motionless against the bottom of the capstan-stand, was raised by the strong arms of her ladyship, who proceeded to detach the hook. Then she carried her as though she had weighed no more than an infant, and laid her upon the sofa on which the two had been previously seated together.

The application of vinegar to her temples, Eau de Cologne to her wrists, and salts to her nostrils, caused Miss Malville to open her eyes, wherein clearly shone the light of reawakened terror and incipient fever. Her pallor was almost the dread pallor of death though by moments it was exchanged for an equally abnormal deep red flush. In a voice of pain, she said:

"My lady, have pity! I cannot breathe. Set me free. I cannot suffer more."

But the cruel mistress, far from showing pity, replied:

"Be silent! You are too talkative! The commencement is painful, I know. But as I have told you, it is necessary to know how to suffer in order to acquire beauty. Your sole thought should now be the regulating of your breathing. It is unnecessary for a woman of society to puff like a grampus. Take in just the amount of air that your lungs require. The discomfort will vanish and you will be as beautiful as a dream. There now, stand up! Like that! Let me help you."

The unfortunate girl, in the hope that the change of position would bring her a measure of relief, had attempted to stand up and had fallen heavily backwards. She now lay at full length on the sofa, just as she had been laid there after her faint by Lady Flayskin.

Assisted by the strong arms of the mistress, Virginia rose in a wooden fashion as though she had no joints. A rumbling was in her ears and the voice of Lady Flayskin came to her as though from the other side of a wall. Her sight was dim and difficult, for blood rushed to her head, giving a look of smouldering fire to her pupils. This look would quickly disappear and the eyes would appear as colourless and expressionless as doubtless did, to their owner, the scene upon which they fell.

Lady Flayskin spoke again.

"You shall see how beautiful you are going to be. This corset fits you perfectly, it makes you appear delicious, dearest. When you have on your dress... no, not the silk one you have taken off... the other one, of muslin, in accordance with the regulations of the establishment... I tell you that when you wear this dress, its waist measure matching that of the corset, and when you look in the glass, you will not recognise yourself... Now you abuse me for making you suffer... You don't deny it? Don't make that pretty gesture of denial; it is needless... The day will come, I tell you, when you will thank me for having taught you how to show of your charms to such perfect advantage."

The poor girl was certainly unable to make any interruption. Her arms felt as heavy as lead and she had not the least desire to make the smallest deprecating gesture. She had, it is true, made a faint effort to join her hands in an attitude of entreaty, but the slight movement had proved beyond her exhausted strength. The chattering of the mistress made her giddy. Every sound echoed in her brain like blows on an anvil.

Lady Flayskin appeared resolved to increase her pupil's discomfort yet farther, for her gestures increased and multiplied in a manner as useless as disagreeable, while, contrary to her wont, she raised her voice until she almost seemed to shout.

"I suppose," she continued, "that I must have a weakness for you, to be spoiling you to such an extent. Here am I passing you your dress after having laced up your corset? Upon my word I am acting like your lady's maid. It is past belief. Tell that to the other pupils! But I flatly forbid you to do any such thing. Will you tell them?"

The girl's lips stirred but no sound did they make. Her mouth felt dry and burning, as did her throat also, for all saliva seemed to have ceased to flow.

Her ladyship insisted. Approaching her mouth to her pupil's ear, she shouted with all her strength:

"Will you kindly do me the honour to reply?"

Virginia trembled as though a thunder bolt had burst in the room. With a grimacing expression of suffering, she forced her lips to utter a sound, and Lady Flayskin received the almost inaudible reply:

"Yes!"

"Yes *what?*"

She made no reply. Her ladyship cried:

"This is insupportable! You now fail in respect to me, who thought your silly pride had been driven out of you. You speak to me as to a lady's maid. I have helped you to dress, it is true, but that is no reason for thinking me the servant of your whims. Servile work is not my work. If I have been disposed to consent to do it, it is because it pleased me. My motive is sufficient and is no extenuation of your bad manners. Reply properly. Or, if not..."

She feigned passionate anger, ground her teeth and shook her fist in the face of the suffering girl, who faintly murmured:

"Yes, my lady."

"Very good! Your dress is now fastened up. Come and look at

yourself in the glass. There!"

She led her along, half pushing her, for in her present condition Virginia was incapable of guiding her steps. She was like a walking statue, her movements being stiff, mechanical, lifeless. The wretched girl was losing all appearance of health and naturalness because she could not find what the rest of humanity finds without searching: breath. And when breath cannot be found, death is not slow in making its appearance.

Virginia was led in front of the tall glass at the end of the room which reflected the full length of her frame, and looking therein she saw something white and misty which was herself. She gazed dully at the muslin dress adorned with the azure-blue sash in accordance with the custom of the school.

The head-mistress insisted upon her admiring herself with enthusiasm:

"Ah! What a slender waist! You outdo my three "Wasps" of whom I am so proud and who arouse admiration wherever I take them. Upon my word, you are better than they! I had said I would make a marvel of you. But how spiritless you are! You are as indifferent as though the matter concerned another person, as though the glass did not reflect your face, your tempting bust, your rounded hips, but merely the charms of another. Come, a little more coquetry! You had too much and now you have not sufficient. It is past belief. A young girt so beautiful as you, unable to raise a smile before her looking-glass!"

But enthusiasm was the last matter of which Virginia felt herself capable. It was the breath of life, for which she feebly sought. It was the burning in her stomach that she would fain have calmed, striving vainly with her ribs to resist the cruel pressure of the unyielding stays. Nothing seemed to her of any moment in comparison with the necessity of escaping from the prison in which her body was held captive, and to have gained such freedom she would willingly have given her beauty of which her mistress was so desirous she should be proud. She had, in truth, been proud of her beauty, but now it seemed to her a burden, responsible for the awful garment she was doomed to wear.

Her ladyship brought back Virginia's thoughts to the full horror of the moment by the announcement of a new torture.

"You do well to refuse to admire your costume, for you have not your gloves. I am becoming as stupid as you. It is true that it is not necessary that I should think of everything. You ought yourself to have thought of them. But here they are. Put them on! Ah! clumsy girl, why do you drop them?"

It was plain that it would have been ridiculous to think Miss Malville capable herself of picking up the gloves which had slipped from her grasp. It was, however, not so evident whether the gloves had been dropped by simple clumsiness on the part of the girl, or whether the mistress, cruel and unnatural to a degree, had not desired that they should fall in order that the sufferings of her unfortunate victim might be increased to her most extreme limit.

She stood a moment in front of the girl and stared into her eyes until she seemed to transfix her pupil with terror.

The latter attempted to go down on her knees, in the hope that without bending her chest, an absolutely impossible action, she might be able to feel about blindly on the ground with her hands to find and pick up the gloves.

Possibly Lady Flayskin rightly estimated the peril of such an attempt and thought matters had been pushed far enough, for she picked up the gloves herself, remarking:

"I am going to put them on you myself, though not of course because you are incapable, as you desire to appear, of doing so yourself unaided, for that I do not think to be the case. This, however, must be the last caprice I can humour, as I warn you."

She raised the hands of the girl and found them as cold and limp as if they had been a doll's. Angrily she exclaimed:

"Stiffen your fingers!"

It seemed as though she had some kind of hypnotic influence over the girl, for her fingers stiffened immediately and the gloves could be put on, tight though they were. The mistress buttoned them dextrously and drew them up in a skilful manner until the arms of their wearer were painfully encased, up to and beyond the elbow, in their creaseless black kid coverings.

It was only a discomfort the more.

Virginia had now no portion of her body at ease. The excessively high heels and tight boots gave her cramping pains in her calves and thighs. Her ribs threatened to crack beneath the corset and now her hands were forced into gloves far too small for them. The easy grace of her movements of which she had formerly been so proud, as befitted an English girl of the aristocratic class devoted to outdoor sports, where now was that grace?

Lost for long days to come!

So confused had become her mind that this thought come to her but dimly.

What occupied her troubled brain was the feeling of giddiness, the racking persistent headache which seemed to fasten talons of steel into her tortured scalp. Lady Flayskin now thought fit to thrust the girl before her into the class-room, that her school-fellows might see her new costume.

CHAPTER VII

It was as the head-mistress had predicted. The slender waist of Miss Malville made a sensation. The glory of the "Three Wasps" was somewhat dimmed.

On Sunday, at church, the men were transfixed with admiration as they looked at the figures of the schoolgirls, while the women went pale with envy. As for us boys, we too shared in these attentions, as owing to our tight-laced corsets, we were likewise taken for girls. Our modest becoming air, our short little steps, the way we had of keeping our eyes lowered, all these and other outward signs aided the deception.

For the present no one had eyes except for Miss Malville, who, in her person, was the embodiment of all the graces due to the inexorable discipline of our establishment — the stays worn night and day, the high boots with their exaggerated heels, the gloves of glazed kid reaching above the elbow.

Lady Flayskin had likewise made her don the "combination," that garment which was bodice and drawers in one, and made of black glazed kid fitting exceedingly tight.

She had been spared the shoulder straps nor had she ever worn the leather collar.

It is true that Virginia carried herself so perfectly upright that these objects would, in her case, have proved absolutely superfluous.

Lady Flayskin was practical before everything. If the carriage of the body was correct, why use artificial aids?

Meanwhile an event of the highest interest took place. It had long been expected and no one was taken by surprise.

One day, the head-mistress announced, in a manner even more ceremonious than that to which we were accustomed, that there would be no school the following day. We were all, boys and girls alike, invited to the wedding of worthy Mr. Gostock with pretty Stella.

The austere, hypocritical old fellow had long meditated this action and his dissimulation had deceived nobody, so true is it that passion always betrays itself. We had one and all expected either a marriage or an elopement and the only thing which surprised us was that one or other of these contingencies had not occurred long ago.

Mr. Gostock was almost an old man and he was marrying a girl who had scarcely had time to greet her sixteenth summer.

In our opinion, he was marrying her less for her grace and prettiness then because she would be so good to whip.

There was reason to believe that the pious American revelled in the pastime of flagellation. He was passionately fond of seeing children whipped and was always on the spot at the precise moment when Stella was about to apply the birch to a rebellious posterior. So soon as the "trussing" of the victim began, he quickly made his way to the best place. Then with eyes which ordinarily seemed dead, mere colourless marble devoid of all expression, and now aflame with a lugubrious light, he literally drank in the scene of suffering. He intoxicated himself with the spectacle, uttering little involuntary yelps of pleasure. There was something repulsive in this greedy satisfaction, and we were terrified and disgusted, though we should have found it difficult to say why, by the sight of him at these moments.

With the natural gaiety of childhood we found that there was more to laugh at than to fear in Mr. Gostock. With great irreverence we would mock his mannerisms and his words. We laughed at his senile passions, his expression of face, and his clothes. Nothing about him escaped our raillery.

His animation always increased as the tears of the victim flowed faster; when the sufferings became more intense and the cries more piercing.

When the punishment was ended, it was Mr. Gostock's wont to congratulate Stella in pompous language which was really ridiculous. He always thought it necessary to allude to the decency and high morality of the proceeding. His face would be as red as a tomato and his trembling hands would shift about here, there, and everywhere. He usually found it necessary to toy affectionately with Stella's chin or to else pat her white arms.

There was nothing astonishing, therefore, in his marrying her.

The ceremony was a notable one. We learnt through the gossip of the servants the real reasons of the marriage, together with certain edifying details regarding the married life of this virtuous man.

He was very rich. It was this fact which decided exceedingly good-looking Stella to accept him as husband and to humour his whims. It may be added that the taste for whipping was shared by both.

The coquetry of this child succeeding in securing a man so ripe in years and so free, on account of his wealth, to choose a partner from any country or station in life which took his fancy, would seem very strange, if due account is not taken of a certain prime factor — astute Lady Flayskin.

The head-mistress had planned to join in indissoluble union these two being so admirably suited for one another. She succeeded without difficulty. Stella understood perfectly her ladyship's directions as to what should and what should not be done in her courting of the American.

Never for a moment had she deviated from the rules laid down for her guidance by Lady Flayskin.

She had become skilled, while keeping her air of childish innocence, in whetting the appetites of Mr. Gostock. The cruelty and science of her chastisements made her irresistible in the eyes of her elderly admirer, and she knew further how to stimulate his feelings by her gestures when her punishments were terminated. She would notice by signs he could never dissimulate that his passions were awakened and she would then as though inadvertently, lay a caressing hand upon the rounded spheres in front of her. At such moments, Mr. Gostock had difficulty in containing himself.

We children had discovered many things during nights spent together in the dormitory. We had even reached the stage of rendering one another certain small services in the presence of the under-mistresses and the directress herself, for we had found that such services were a very great relief to the feelings after a painful flogging. We knew the best medicine for poor smarting, itching thighs, and the whip always had upon us a certain nervous effect. It was due to this knowledge that we perfectly understood that the actions and gestures of Stella for all her attractive air of a innocence, were only a piquant preface. We were able to follow all the stages of Stella's treatment without difficulty, the American's looks and movements betraying all to our childish but discerning eyes.

This Puritan was a widower.

By his first marriage he had had, and still had a troop of children, the eldest of whom was twelve and the youngest five. He had left them in America in the charge of a woman — a saint as he was wont to say in whom he could repose entire confidence.

Ah! his confidence was well placed! She was in effect a holy woman, after the heart of the respectable Yankee. By her vicious practices, the pious dame had taught bad habits to the three boys. Then, under the pretence of punishing them, she had obliged them to behave in the presence of their father in the manner they behaved when alone. Naturally such *séances* ended in terrible collective floggings.

During the lifetime of his first wife, Mr. Gostock had had carnal intercourse with this holy woman. She had grown old and Mr. Gostock saw Stella at work and had be come enamoured of the girl. He counted upon her to punish his boys and see to the education of his daughters.

He was not disappointed in his hopes.

As I have already frequently had occasion to remark, everything became known that transpired in the mysterious establishment of Lady Flayskin. Tongues were not idle. Voices were not raised high, but they talked none the less for all that. Our sharp ears surprised every happening. The girlish education and costume seemed to arouse in us boys a feminine appetite for scandal and gossip.

If means of information as to what was happening about us were otherwise lacking we found in the servants' gossip all we sought. It was for the most part perfectly reliable, for the servants, like other members of the humbler classes, did not believe that any embellishments proceeding from their own simple brains could make truth more wonderful or interesting.

They would tell what they knew, in the course of conversation, to the elder pupils who naturally found nothing better to do than to repeat what they had learnt to the younger children.

The stories would go the round of the school and, contrary to gossip in a bigger world, did not vary nor grow as it passed from mouth to mouth.

In this way we were kept fully informed of the doings of the little world about us.

Thus, too, we learnt what happened in Mr. Gostock's new home.

The day after his wedding, the American decided that he could not occupy himself better than in beating his children. The scene was the dining-room at the hour of dinner. He found that all of them were in fault and to each addressed a reproof, although not one of the poor children was to blame. Since the death of their mother, they had been in the habit of paying trembling attention to their good conduct. Deprived for long of all affection or tenderness, very unhappy in the charge of the woman to whom their father had entrusted them, they hoped to find in their stepmother something of that love and maternal devotion they so sadly missed.

Children readily believe appearances and believe in the goodness of those they find young and beautiful to look at. For children, fine appearances are a rich source of deception, though it is true some carry their delusions on this score with them through their riper years.

The poor children, fork in hand, now listened to the slow measured tones of their austere-visaged father who told them many things they found disagreeable to hear, together with a plentiful sprinkling of such word as decency and morality!

Malicious Stella had immediately understood to what such observations, addressed by her husband to his children by first wife, were intended to lead.

As she spoke, the children were charmed by her pure crystal tones, and feeling reassured, they turned their attention anew to their plates.

Alas! they were greatly in error.

What pretty Stella proposed to her virtuous husband was simply to flog, there and then, the bare bottoms of all these brats.

"They really merit a flogging on account their behaviour at table," she said. "It is plain that they have been brought up deplorably and if the whip is not immediately applied we shall have a great deal of trouble with them in future. We shall no be able to have our meals in peace with the children at the table. We shall have to be continually employing cross words. In my opinion the children of so respected a father should have good principles instilled into them, and the sooner the better, in order that as they grow up, they may be respected in their turn. If you have no objection, we will begin immediately?"

The wretched old fellow felt his cup of joy running over as he saw his wishes so perfectly understood. He felt that this was indeed a fit realisation of the dream his heart had nursed so long. Kissing the hands of his sweet young wife, he told her that she was mistress in her own house and begged her to do as she thought for the best.

Thereupon, doubtless with the object of heightening her husband's amorous desires and giving him further joy, vicious Stella fell into his arms as though transported with gratitude and rewarded him with a long, affectionate kiss.

Then she went to the collection of birch rods in a corner of the room, and chose from among them those which appeared most suitable. Stella possessed to an admirable degree a sense of proportion. Accordingly, for the elder children she chose thick and heavy rods, while for the smaller her choice was made from among the slender and tapering bunches of birch.

All therefore were whipped, beginning at the eldest and concluding with the youngest, tears and protestations making not the smallest difference in their sufferings. Each child after being whipped, had to ask papa's pardon and promise to be good in future. The penitent had to go upon his or her knees with face turned to the wall. In this position, the little girls had to hold up, with both hands, their chemise and petticoats, while the little boys whose knickerbockers were about their ankles had to similarly raise their shirt-tails. In this position they had to remain until the end of the meal. Their choking sobs and stifled wails of suffering agreeably supplied the place of skilled musicians, in the opinion of virtuous

Mr. Gostock. From time to time he cast his eyes along the row of bruised, scarred sterns, this exhibition of the flesh of his flesh so pitilessly beaten. His face would then light up with a smile of content while he kissed the fair hands of his adorable young bride.

This scene, alternated with others — for lovely Stella's imagination matched her intelligence — was often re-enacted.

For the rest, Mr. Gostock had only to let fall a word to find it immediately under stood by his wife, who deferred to his every passing whim to the despair of the hindquarters of the puny members of his household.

Not only had Mr. Gostock made arrangements in his will whereby everything which by law had not to revert to his children should fall to his wife, but he had further (so skilled was he in legal chicanery) managed to despoil his lawful heirs of nearly all their legal inheritance in favour of this second wife so greatly and unfairly favoured.

In exchange, Stella gave him all the happiness one can hope for on this earth when united to a lawful wife and awaiting a better world — that paradise where doubtless, for the joy of virtuous Americans, the angels whip little children.

But I have anticipated. It is difficult to be as orderly in one's narrative as in one's ideas, more especially in the case of a narrative opening out so many attractive bypaths as the present.

I return therefore, after this digression, to the marriage rejoicings of Mr. Gostock. We were all, boys and girls alike, as I have said, invited, and we were in charge of the head-mistress.

Early in the morning, we all, servants, pupils and governesses, took our places in two breaks, drawn, each of them, by four horses to the gay music of two energetic posthorn players. The populace of the villages rushed to their doors and gates to see us pass, attracted by the music and the horses. We were flattered by the remarks of the country wenches, women and their husbands, and by the cries of exclamation or admiration of the pleasure in the somewhat sour, unmistakably envious looks of the elder girls. We had no need to hold our heads as though we had been supplied with bearing-reins. We did not wear the cruel leather collar, but our stays kept our figures in excellent shape and very erect. It is hardly necessary to say that all corsets had been laced under the eye of the head-mistress and that her ladyship had paid particular attention to the operation.

The nine miles which separated us from Mr. Gostock's house at Faversham were covered in an hour and a quarter.

Of the actual ceremony I shall say nothing except that, as always, our waists did not fail to attract considerable attention. After the service, fine ladies fingered and felt the "Three Wasps" and asked them questions. The replies were dictated by what they knew to be their head-mistress's wishes, otherwise their questioners would have received some strange revelations. The young ladies, it is unnecessary to add, made their answers with perfect politeness and amiability.

Lady Flayskin's prediction was realised. The triumph of the "Three Wasps" was as nothing in comparison with that of Miss Virginia Malville.

Virginia had paid dearly for her glory. Interminable sleepless nights were only a part of the price she paid for the admiration and astonishment aroused by a waist whose like had never hitherto been seen.

The head-mistress had spared no pains with this unique example of the power of corset discipline.

The corset! Dread word whose meaning the poor girl at length thoroughly understood! In the morning before she rose, Virginia was wont to receive three visitors, the head-mistress and those two strong-armed servants whose task it had been on the day of Virginia's first flogging to thrust her back into the class-room.

These visitors would find the girl relapsing into a short, fitful slumber after a night of weariness and wakefulness.

It was necessary that she should rise. Her night-corset was taken off in order that her day-corset might be put on. In the evening, when retiring to rest, the same persons paid their visit and performed the contrary operation.

At these visits, the head-mistress would measure, calculate and take careful note of the effects of the lacing on the ever diminishing size of the pupil's waists.

The night-corset was scarcely in any respect different from the day-corset. The former however, was of strong linen, instead of brocaded silk. Its busks and whalebones were less stiff and unyielding and close than in the case of the day-corset. But as regarded the sole particular which aroused any interest in the victim, the lacing, in both cases, remained the same.

The same set of rules sufficed for the other boys and girls of the school. In the case of the "Three Wasps," and Virginia Malville, there was a special and severe code. It was upon Virginia that these regulations of a severer order weighed heaviest. Both as regards her corset, boots, and gloves, the head-mistress was pitiless. No relaxation of their discipline was ever permitted in Virginia's case.

To do justice to the truth, it must be acknowledged that the girl so attired had a very distinguished and attractive appearance.

Her tallness was accentuated by her high heels. Her sculptural leg and aristocratic foot were shown to their very best advantage in the arched boots reaching up the leg as far as the swelling calf. Her fine sloping shoulders and classic throat gained a perfection of outline (if such had previously been lacking) from the corset compressing the waist to a space easily encircled by the ten fingers. Her plump arm showed a glimpse of its pure white satin beauty just above the elbow where the long, black kid glove ended. Her hand was long and slender, that of a lady of noble birth skilled in the weaving of tapestry. One could imagine a hunting-glove worn to protect those tapering fingers from the fierce falcon poised upon my lady's wrist as her champing palfrey bore her to the chase.

Had Lord Malville seen his daughter at this moment, he would certainly have been astonished, proud, and happy.

Formerly the haughty girl had shown herself conscious of her charms. It was not so now. The difficulty of breathing was now the only thing of which she thought, for so soon as she became in the least degree used to any measurement in her stays, the head-mistress gave directions that the lacing should be tighter.

Where would matters stop?

We all asked the question, though with more curiosity than pity. Each of us had sufficient personal discomfort to put up with without thinking too much about Miss Malville's troubles, however real they might be to that young lady.

The girl was forced to veil her feelings in a constant smile, for such was the head-mistress's desire. She ordained that smile in tones there was no disputing. It was necessary to smile.

Virginia was of a deathly pallor whose ghastliness every now and then alternated with the deep red flush which would involuntarily rise to her cheeks to prove her sufferings. From time to time, she coughed and, when she thought she was unobserved, spat into her handkerchief, her expectoration betraying a thin streak of blood. Then she would smile perpetually, like one of those panting ballet-girls, also laced tightly in torturing corsets while going through their violent exercises. They always appear content, whether they are balancing on the tips of their toes, or submitting after their exertions to the cold draughts of the stage or greenroom. For the spectators they have always the same delighted smile.

Poor Virginia, whose *rôle* was so similar, had, at the expense of her own feelings and sufferings, to make a parade of joy for the benefit of Lady Flayskin and for the pleasure of the aristocratic circles with whom the directress's influence and popularity were of so pronounced a nature.

After dinner, a meal magnificently served, as befitted the occasion and the great wealth of the bridegroom, we were taken to a large room which was afterwards to be our dormitory for the night. Here we washed ourselves and made as perfect a toilet as was possible. Lady Flayskin's severe and vigilant eye was upon us, all the time, nor did that lady fail to improve the occasion by lecturing us in her usual half sermonizing, half reprimanding manner.

She told us that at this evening's party we should see represented all the families of the neighbourhood, the very cream of local society. All were anxious to pay a tribute of respect to Mr. Gostock on his wedding day, and a tribute of admiration to the pupils of Lady Flayskin's establishment who were known to be among the guests.

Lady Flayskin asked us, parenthetically, to admire the mysterious ways of Providence, who had, so to speak, taken Mr. Gostock by the hand and conducted him to the celebrated establishment of which we were members, with the sole aim of enabling him to appreciate the solid and excellent qualities of Miss

Stella and of thus deciding him to make that young lady his lawful wife in the presence of God and men.

Here Lady Flayskin closed her parenthesis, but thought it fitting to commence another immediately. With lowered voice and finger laid upon her lips, looking about with an air of extraordinary discretion and circumspection, she informed us that Stella had been but a poor orphan, but that she, Lady Flayskin, had discovered her nascent sterling qualities when the girl was only ten years old.

This example of evangelistic charity next served her ladyship as text for a discourse upon the beauties of the discipline of the corset, gloves and high-heeled high boots, in short upon all the virtues of kid. She, however, omitted to allude to the virtues of the rod, prime cause of the good fortune of whipping Stella.

She further earnestly exhorted us to be polite and well-mannered, as befitted guests in such distinguished company. She added (and thought it fitting at this part of her discourse to assume an enigmatic smile) that if the corset of Stella had made so marvellous a conquest, there was room to hope that all the other young ladies, whose corsets were similarly tight-laced, would be similarly fortunate. As to be the boys, she said, marriage was not for the present to occupy their juvenile thoughts. They must, however, strive this evening, by their modest mien and becoming conduct, to show themselves worthy of the establishment whose privileges they were permitted to enjoy, and of the feminine costume in which that establishment's regulations, for their highest good and in their best interests, thought fit to clothe them.

After this curious speech, which had lasted a good half-hour by the clock, permission was given us to walk in the garden. We accordingly gratefully accepted this pleasure and I noticed in Mr. Gostock's fine park many a blackbird's and thrush's nest which I should doubtless have attempted to secure had my garments been in the least degree those of a boy.

For that matter, neither boys nor girls thought of playing any of the games or indulging in any of the occupations natural to their age. Our costume forbade any such indulgence, and we only thought of such relaxations to regret our incapacity to take part therein. How could we run or jump with these narrow boots, these inconvenient high heels; how could the skipping-rope be used when this terrible corset was worn? After every leap, our intestines would infallibly have been reduced to mere pulp. How could we play at leapfrog while wearing these close-fitting drawers? Even the simple humble hoop was denied us, for it would have endangered the bursting of our gloves which we were stringently forbidden to take off.

We therefore walked in little groups down the shady paths, occupied in the sole amusement in which we were free to indulge, that of gossip and scandal mongering.

It was either the effect of the corset, that garment whose eulogy we were weary of hearing and whose moral and physical influence was so deleterious, it was either, I say, this, or the example we ever had before us in our bitter-tongued directress, but in any case — be the cause what it might — we showed ourselves on this day thorough little hypocrites in the perfidy and the honeyed virulence of our remarks. In this respect, the boys were not a whit behind the girls. Each of us was skilled alike in stabbing with the tongue; each of us, upon this occasion, showed what talons could be concealed beneath a velvet paw; what fangs behind the sweetness of a smile.

It was the corset which added years to our young shoulders, and turned little boys into elderly *roués* or repulsive caricatures of the opposite sex.

In the case of both girls and boys, the chief preoccupation was this accursed corset. We were proud of our slender waists. We could not find terms sufficiently mocking or contemptuous to describe women unconnected with our establishment. What sacks they were! How heavy! How thick! We found the prettiest of girls to be common-looking, graceless and shapeless. It did not even occur to us, so taken up were we with our own elegance, as we thought it to be, that others would have been precisely as we, had they too passed through the skilled hands of Lady Flayskin, the champion of corset discipline.

Thus came about the natural but disastrous result that we grew to love the chains which bound us.

For the girls there remained some hope. But the boys!

In our case, it was ruin absolute and final; that canker which gnaws into all succeeding years. All desire to wrestle for and gain our meed of honour in the battle of life was stifled for ever in these early days. We were left feeble and disarmed, unfit to struggle or even compete with strong and resolute men, nerveless, bloodless warriors in the merciless clash and clang of existence where the strong man wins and the weak man goes to the wall.

A deep-noted gong signalled to us to make our way to the drawing-room. We were soon joined there by the other guests.

We found ourselves, as our head-mistress had told us would be the case, in the society of eminently *chic* persons. There were old gentlemen of Mr. Gostock's respectable antiquity, but, curious to relate, not a single middle-aged man. There were young girls whose corsets and gloves resembled our own in tightness, and beautifully-dressed ladies. When however, I drew nearer to one of the girls I found that she belonged to my own sex.

A boy?

What could that mean?

I felt extremely curious and was on the point of making a commonplace remark to the young person with the object of beginning an interesting dialogue when I jumped nearly out of my skin. The voice of the head-mistress sounded in my ears:

"Alice! Come here!"

I had been watched! Trembling, I obeyed.

"Sit down there, and do not move a muscle. It is not your place to begin a conversation."

But I was used to Lady Flayskin's ingenious discoveries of punishable offences and used also to failing to understand the justice of the penance prescribed.

I was therefore resigned to the necessity of seating myself with a good grace on the edge of the chair indicated, for with our abominable stays it was impossible to think of leaning back, and had we attempted such a feat we should never have been able to raise ourselves again. I assumed as modest and penitent a mien as I was able and consoled myself with the thought that after all we were guests and no doubt I had inadvertently transgressed some mysterious rule of etiquette. My only fear was lest the head-mistress should revert to the matter on our return to school and make a mountain out of it. She was not the person to forget any matter whether little or big.

Any illusions I might have cherished in this connection were doomed to be swiftly dissipated.

Refreshments were brought in. Champagne frothed and was poured into glasses and then down throats, after the manner of champagne. The animation was at its highest, when Lady Flayskin, always, to employ a vulgarism, on the spot at important moments, proposed the first toast. She made a long, flowery speech regarding conjugal felicity, the excellent choice the universally esteemed Mr. Gostock had made, and the no less enduring than brilliant qualities of his bride. Then she announced:

"For you, dear child, I have reserved a pleasant surprise. I have had to reprimand some of my pupils, but their punishment has not yet taken place and I have counted upon you to apply it. Do not refuse me this kindness before we separate. I earnestly desire to see some impertinent hinder hemispheres whipped by you who know so well the science of the rod."

Pretty Stella's eyes were illumined by pleasurable anticipation and also, no doubt, by the effects of the champagne and other exciting delights of the day. Rising from her chair, she replied:

"Why, certainly! I will do what you request with real delight: It is actually some days since I have whipped a boy or girl on — ahem! — the part destined by nature to receive chastisement. My arm is well rested and woe betide the posteriors destined to taste its vigour. I can promise them full measure. They will afterwards be able to boast of the excellent good-bye spanking they received on this memorable occasion. Please tell me who is to be the first and I will begin at once."

It was with stupefaction, as the reader may imagine, that I heard this speech and what with my fear and my stays, I could scarcely draw my breath. I was somewhat relieved, however, by the head-mistress's rejoinder.

"Begin with Dora. I reprimanded her yesterday and have specially reserved the chastisement of her behind for you to-day."

Dora with a piercing shriek attempted to escape to the garden. Servants, however, had been posted at the door. They caught the child and brought her back.

Dora was a sweet, fair-haired, pink-cheeked girl, as appetising as cream, (alas, she was about to be converted into whipped cream!) with dimples everywhere. Her stays literally cut her in two. Her waist was of extraordinary slenderness, which made the well-developed bust and large hips appear the more pronounced.

Nimble-fingered Stella "trussed" her in the twinkling of an eye in spite of her tears, cries, and efforts to resist. Her petticoats were pinned to her shoulders, revealing large hinder spheres black and shining, for naturally, Dora like the rest of us, wore the horrible, close-fitting drawers of black kid.

The beating of the rod upon this vast rump was like the rolling of drums. As I listened to her agonised shrieks and prayers for pity, I knew but too well what was in store for my own latter end.

"And the next?" inquired hateful Stella, as she let Dora go. The victim had certainly received an over-dose.

"It is Alice's turn, if you will be so obliging," replied the head-mistress.

"If I will be so obliging? Why I shall be charmed! I have always found special delight in whipping the impertinent seat of that vicious little boy. His back parts tremble in such a curious, interesting manner."

Seeing "Alice," that is to say myself, dressed, of course, like a girl and pushed towards Stella by the servants, some of the old gentlemen were moved by the strongest curiosity. I heard them murmur:

"Look! Look!"

It was certainly an unusual spectacle, this big boy of ten years old walking awkwardly forward, equally troubled by the curious looks, his stays, his high heels and the other feminine paraphernalia, as by his fear of the scene which was, he knew, to follow. They saw me throw myself upon my knees and with clasped hands implore Stella to intercede for me, and afterwards, since the entreaty fell upon deaf ears, implore her not to strike me too hard. They saw Stella laugh until tears run down her cheeks, then truss me. They saw the exact form and configuration of my hindquarters for, boy though I was, I wore the black kid drawers, tight and shining, which have been so frequently described.

They saw, too, the ridiculous trembling movements adored by Stella, for I had my reasons for shaking my poor curves beneath the torment. Ah, the wretch! Never did she whip with a more perfect mastery of her art. To say good-bye, she wrote an unforgettable "P. P. C." upon my martyred beam-end.

The old gentlemen saw that for me all feelings of shame were of no account, so great was my pain and terror.

All these things they could see and hear and it appears that they both looked and listened with prodigious amusement and satisfaction. Possibly their senile lusts were stimulated by the scene? Ah, the monsters!

On being permitted to regain my chair, I seated myself astride across the seat, forgetful of my skirts and, resting my arms upon the chair's back, buried my face in my shame and misery, crying as though my heart would break.

This was a fresh opportunity for the mirth of the company who did not fail to take advantage of it.

I suddenly heard the voice of Lady Flayskin pronounce my name in tones sharper and more bitter than verjuice.

"Alice!"

I quickly assumed a more feminine attitude, especially as I had had another reminder of my momentary forgetfulness, even more disagreeable than the voice of her ladyship. In leaning forward over the chair's back, I had broken one of my staybusks. A sharp end consequently stuck into my stomach, causing me horrible agony. I dared not make a movement now.

Conversation was resumed. The company appeared to be in excellent, even tumultuous, spirits. The ingredients for making punch were brought in.

Mr. Gostock stepped forward in his usual solemn manner and undertook to superintend the mixing. Night had fallen, but Stella declared that obscurity in the room would be vastly more amusing than artificial light. Naturally the wishes of the little chit were laws for her husband, and darkness accordingly reigned, broken by the flickering green and blue flames from the ignited rum, uncertain ghoulish dimness.

In this half-light, transpired scenes of an extraordinary nature. Mistresses and servants circulated swiftly among us pupils and in less time almost than it takes to relate, had stripped us naked, boys and girls alike, in spite of our resistance and cries. I said "naked," but I should explain that for the moment they did not remove that black, glazed kid combination, the skin-tight garment which revealed, rather than concealed our youthful forms, nor our stockings, or high-heeled boots.

We were pushed towards the table on which stood the flaming punchbowl and each of us was bidden to drink amid those infernal flames to the health of the bride.

How long drinking and singing continued, I hardly know. Nor do I know to what cause to attribute the strangely lascivious desires nor the mad excitement which transformed the girls into furies and the boys into satyrs.

Had the punch been drugged?

Had the moral American, highly respected Mr. Gostock, president of numerous societies for the promotion of public morality, mingled therein stimulating cantharides or some potent phosphoric acid? I know not. The fact remains that our movements became of the wildest and most unbridled order. The strangest fancies seized us in a grip there was no resisting and drew us, unwilling and yet willing, towards a seething vortex of obscenity that absorbed us, sucked us down, one and all.

No pen can write what passed in Stella's drawing-room on the evening of her wedding day. No writer would dare to paint in detail that unforgettable night of triumphant vice, that mad delirium which cast us into the arms of grizzled patriarchs, which gave us naked, yet unashamed, into the hands, sheathed in black glazed kid, of fair society ladies...

CHAPTER VIII

Eight months!

Eight months have already passed since the death of my father. I still wear mourning for him and I still wear the dishonouring garb of Lady Flayskin's highly select establishment.

Seven months have passed since I slept under this roof for the first time.

Sometimes during the night, stifled laughter from the girl's dormitory comes through the thin partition and awakes me. I fall again into a fitful slumber disturbed by bad dreams. I think I am being done to death by a goblin who sits upon my body and gnaws it. I awake and find that the busk of my corset is sticking into my stomach.

My neighbour's voice comes to me in a whisper from the next bed.

"Will you play?" he asks.

Although I reply in the negative, he raises my bedclothes and slips into my bed. I am obliged to submit silently to his repugnant contact, for should I occasion a quarrel, my companion would perhaps receive the whip and I should certainly be flogged.

For such was the "distributive justice" of Lady Flayskin.

Nor did she ever fail in her preliminary lectures to insert some fine sentiments regarding the duties of *bonne camaraderie*.

I shudder yet as I think of the deeds that fair-sounding expression was employed to cover in the Flayskin Academy. And many a sun has set since those far-off days.

One memorable morning, a servant entered the school-room with a note for Mrs. Stuart.

The mistress put her spectacles on her thin nose and read the short missive with an air of astonishment. I saw her read it through a second time and then sign to Mrs. Eagle who likewise showed extreme surprise at the communication. I was idly contrasting the leanness of Mrs. Stuart with the plumpness of Mrs. Eagle, who never resembled an eagle less than at that moment, in her goggle-eyed, red-cheeked astonishment, when I heard my name called by the thin governess.

"Jimmy, come here!"

Had a thunderbolt burst at my feet, I could hardly have felt more astonishment than I did at that moment. For seven months I had not been addressed by my own boyish name. Why was I not "Alice?" Why was I a boy again?

So intense were my feelings, that I found it impossible to do otherwise than burst into tears. I made no attempt to obey the summons. My schoolfellows laughed, but I did not mind that. What could it mean?

My attitude was naturally a source of curiosity to my class, but actually aroused no severe reprimand on the part of the governesses whose order I had completely ignored. Finally Mrs. Eagle, after renewed consultation with Mrs. Stuart, came to me. The fat little creature appeared in a state of great excitement and proceeded to bundle me out of the schoolroom.

Leading me through the corridors and upstairs to the dormitory, she proceeded to undress me with much show of haste. I resigned myself to this treatment with very good grace, but hardly knew if I was awake or dreaming when a servant entered with a parcel containing all the garments I had worn on entering the school, when still a boy. I saw the broad-toed serviceable shoes in which I had run so fast in other days, excellent, strong and comfortable shoes. Then I saw my knickerbockers and my little sailor's reefer and cap.

Great Heavens! My own clothes once more! Those I had worn eight months ago! Am I going to wear again?

Such were the thoughts that coursed through my brain. In reply to all my questionings and doubtings, I found that Mrs. Eagle was helping me to put on these clothes, *my clothes*, instead of those hated one I had just taken off. The shoes are a little short, as the abominable narrow, high-heeled boots have lengthened my foot. But no matter! The knickerbockers no longer reach to my knees. But again, what matters, that? What too does it matter, if the sleeves of the little jacket no longer cover my wrists?

Ah, what joy!

Mrs. Eagle becomes momentarily more bustling and excited and her tongue wags faster and faster. It is "dear Jimmy, my darling little Jimmy," my own name repeated so frequently that I begin once more to recognise it as my very own. There is no fear of my being addressed as "Jimmy" and forgetting to answer now. But why? Oh, why?

I decide that Mrs. Eagle is, after all, a good sort. I feel disposed to kiss her, but dare not. She, however, guesses my thoughts and imprints loud, smacking kisses first upon one cheek and then on the other, such kisses as our maid had given me long ago when my father was still alive.

At length my dressing is finished. I find the sailor cap uncomfortable, and think it must have shrunk or else that some paper has been inserted in the lining to make it smaller. But how stupid I am! My head has grown! Great Cæsar! And I laugh heartily as I pull with both hands the obstinate cap and only succeed in exposing the back of my head when I manage to cover the front. Mrs. Eagle also laughs and remarks:

"Little Jimmy, you are going to be even happier presently. A pleasant surprise is in store for you."

But this piece of news has the effect of immediately damping my high sprits. I know the pleasant surprises of Lady Flayskin only too well. They always finish disagreeably.

Mrs. Eagle can make nothing of my sudden change of mien.

"Ah, no! Not by any means! I can't have you going into the drawing-room with that sad face. Oh! certainly not, it's not to be thought of. Why, you must look happy, very happy!"

But happiness cannot be produced to order, and my step, so unpleasantly apprehensive of the promised surprise, became more and more laggard. I finish by coming to a dead stop near the drawing-room.

Mrs. Eagle, however, hurries me forward and adds to my astonishment by neglecting a most important detail of the etiquette of the establishment.

She enters Lady Flayskin's august presence and that lofty person's magnificent drawing-room, without previously knocking at the door and waiting for an invitation to enter. She pushes me in front of her and closes the door.

With a great sigh of joy, I found that my dear mother was there. Almost fainting with delight, I rushed into her arms and covered her dear face with kisses. She returned my kisses with interest and we both of us cried. She hugged me to her breast with almost feverish delight. Then suddenly she held me at arm's length from her and, looking at me earnestly, cried:

"Goodness!" How pale you are!"

Lady Flayskin intervened in honeyed tones.

"It is very natural, dear Madam; a result to be expected from emotion and joy at seeing his mother. You love your mother dearly, don't you, Jimmy?"

"Yes! Oh! Yes!"

I plucked at my mother's dress to take her away with me outside those dreadful walls. I kissed her again and murmured in her ear before removing my mouth:

"You will take me away, won't you? Oh, promise! You will not leave me here?"

She replied aloud:

"Certainly, I shall not leave you. I have come to take you home."

A second time she held me from her and said, as though talking to herself:

"He had such bonnie big cheeks, and now they are hollow. His eyes are burning with fever. You have been ill, my poor mite!"

I burst into sobs and Lady Flayskin hastened to anticipate a possible reply on my part.

"Why, Madam, you surely do not imagine he has been deprived of anything he could wish for? The cooking is excellent; the food wholesome and abundant. I never let my pupils want for anything. Our dear Jimmy will not tell his mother a story? You have always eaten as much as you liked, haven't you, Jimmy?"

"Oh, yes!"

But covertly I pulled my mother's skirt and looked at her with imploring eyes.

She understood me. The dear angel! She has always understood what I have said to her in the dumb language of the eyes.

She rose and took a somewhat ceremonious farewell of Lady Flayskin. Meanwhile, I also turned critic but said nothing. I was none the less astonished and grieved to find my poor mother looking much older. The corners of her lips drooped and her eyelids were swollen and lined as though she had cried a great deal. She also had lost her full, plump, pretty cheeks. It was another and a thinner Mamma I was looking at.

It seemed to me that she would never come to the end of her somewhat cold, but none the less elaborate thanks and compliments. For my part, I should have preferred giving Lady Flayskin a good beating and I pulled at my mother's skirt in a frenzied way.

She turned and smiled.

"Yes! we are going! Say good-bye, Jimmy! Never forget your manners."

"Precisely!" rejoined the horrid old cat. "That is what we always tell our pupils. Jimmy, you do not kiss me?"

How much rather would I have strangled her? Nevertheless, I managed to kiss her and we left the room. The affectation and ceremony of our leave-taking continued, however, until we reached the front door, where at the bottom of the steps a cab awaited us.

It was a hansom cab. Again I have before my eyes, as on that never- to-be-forgotten day, the honest-looking, stout driver with his red whiskers. Again I see him touching his hat as we appear, when he took his short clay pipe from his mouth.

How delightful it was to be in that hansom, nestled against my mother's heart. It gave me a certain feeling of satisfaction and security, too, to think of our stout good-natured coachman perched up there behind us. Would Lady Flayskin try to take me back? In that case, I thought our cabby will not let her. He will make but a mouthful of her and her whole crew of whipping-women and stay-lacers.

What joy to breath the pure air without having to be apprehensive of bones and steel busks sticking into one's stomach and stifling one's lungs!

And how delightful to visit again old scenes and think of the happy rambles and merry games of days past!

Such were my thoughts when, though I hardly know why, I burst into sobs and told my mother everything. The corset, the girl's dress, the high heels, the long tight gloves, all the diabolical "discipline" of glazed black kid, everything was told. Nor did I, the reader may be sure, omit to mention that my name had been "Alice".

My mother cried too, but suddenly laughed, and clapping her hands, told me that Mr. Baker had died eight days before and left her his entire fortune. Consequently, we were very rich. Then, for the first time, I noticed that she was in mourning.

Her face became thoughtful. A world of sorrow was reflected in her beautiful eyes, but she cried no more.

I detested even the memory of Mr. Baker, the cruel stepfather who had been the cause of all my troubles, and I felt inclined to shout with joy at the knowledge that he was dead. But my mother, I thought, must miss him sadly, so I respected her pensive looks and sat back silently in my corner, always however keeping hold of her hand.

Grown-up people so frequently misinterpret each other's sentiments that there is nothing surprising in a child making a similar error. It was only later that I fully understood the reason of those painful reveries which I had mistaken for sorrow.

My poor dear mother did not mourn in her heart for Mr. Baker, although she wore black clothes. She had suffered more at the hands of that monster than I had myself in my horrid school.

My poor mother also had had to submit to the most cruel tight-lacing, as well as to every one of the other tortures I knew so well. Her neck had been almost dislocated, and a doctor had actually been summoned after an excessive use of the "collar". And my dear pretty mother had been whipped; flogged daily and mercilessly, sometimes by Mr. Baker himself and sometimes by that execrable Betsy in his presence. Any pretext, or no pretext, sufficed as a reason for these inflictions.

In the superb Portland Place mansion there was even a special "Punishment Room." On my stepfather's death, my mother locked the door of this grim apartment and it was only some years afterwards that I could inspect it.

Nothing had been disturbed; no one had entered the room since it had been locked up. The first object I noticed was a wooden vaulting horse similar to those employed in gymnasiums, except for the addition of a blood-red pad of kid, highly glazed, and of two steel rings on each side of the neck, so to speak, of the apparatus. It was upon this pad that my dear mother was twisted by Mr. Baker and Betsy. Lying on her stomach, her arms were made fast to the rings and any resistance during her whipping was thus rendered impossible. Her skirts were then pinned over her head and the flogging proceeded with. Some times an immense whip, such as is employed by trainers and others with ungovernable stallions, was used, and sometimes the simple, but exceedingly painful birch rod.

Should the fancy take them, they would "spread-eagle" my dear mother up on a stand designed for the purpose. This apparatus appeared particularly diabolical.

There were pullies, cords, rings, a trapeze and many other such arrangements and objects. The monster had dazzled my mother's eyes with his wealth and she had married him to be tortured by his passions.

It appears that sometimes he had made her run quite naked from end to end of this "Punishment Room" which was but a corridor. As she ran, the long lash of a whip would pursue her, and since the passage did not permit, owing to its narrowness, of side blows, Mr. Baker would strike vertically, either downwards or upwards. In the case of the latter movement, the thighs and stomach received the most severe punishment.

My poor mother would fly shrieking before the pursuing lash. If she fell, a hurricane of blows descended upon her shoulders, back, and lower parts. In spite of her groans, the unfortunate woman would be compelled to rise to her feet and provide fresh sport for the ruffian.

Mr. Baker would further compel his wife to become, so to speak, a horse, and cut capers as though in a circus, always, of course, to the tune of a long-lashed whip.

It appeared that Mr. Baker, like Lady Flayskin, was a devotee of black glazed kid. Consequently, my mother wore gloves of that material and so tight that she could not close her hands. She also wore the abominable tight-fitting combination of chemise and drawers.

But morally she had to endure even more humiliating persecution.

Baker would sometimes install Betsy in his wife's place at table and the latter would take the servant's place as waiting woman. The coarse and vicious drab would heap ridicule upon her and abuse her for clumsiness or any other fancied offence which occurred to them. They would then compel my mother to adopt a pose at once silly and obscene, while before her eyes they kissed and caressed one another in a fashion which can only be described by the one word: shameful.

My mother was allowed no personal liberty. She was not permitted to communicate with any person outside the house, nor could she go out walking or shopping except on the rare occasions when Baker or Betsy consented to accompany her. She could neither receive nor send letters, except after a censorship so cruel on the part of this man that she might as well have been entirely cut off from the rest of the world.

During this period, she was permitted to receive my letters occasionally, but as I myself was unable to write independently of the head-mistress's supervision, she never learnt in that way any of the truth about myself. My letters were dictated, one and all, by astute Lady Flayskin. My mother, however, possessed not only that feminine intuition which so often counts for far more than blind and halting reason; she possessed also in no common degree a passion of maternal love whose pure flame had seemed to be actually fed at the altar of her own sufferings. Thankful, indeed, she was to know, from seeing my writing, that I still lived, but her heart told her that all was not well, that I too suffered.

But what could she do? She could, and did pour out her heart to the Most High and awaited the intervention of that Providence whose ways are mysterious.

Her prayers were not unheeded. We were reunited, rich in the world's possessions and free of our bodies as of our minds.

Mr. Baker's death had been sudden. A confirmed and immoderate spirit-drinker, he had one evening indulged in a certain fiery Scotch whiskey to an extent unusual ever with him. Under the influence of the alcohol, his savage passions of cruelty and lust were aroused and he ordered my mother to the Punishment Room.

His unfortunate victim, well aware from long experience that resistance was worse than useless, obeyed. Betsy accompanied her and on the staircase dealt her a cruel box on the ears with the object, as the low creature averred of making her mend her face.

My poor mother was then stripped of her clothes by the same coarse and cruel hands and bound to the wooden apparatus covered with glazed red kid. The heavy, unsteady steps of the drunkard then approached from the dining-room.

Tottering into the Punishment Room, Baker selected the long-lashed trainer's whip and managed to crack it once or twice, as was his wont, with the purpose of inspiring due preliminary terror in the heart of his victim. Suddenly he stumbled, the whip fell from his hands, and he would have fallen to the ground had not Betsy received him in her arms.

Alcoholic congestion and Neronic excitement had done their work.[2]

Seeing her master without breath or movement, Betsy completely lost her head. Forgetting even to free my mother who was stretched over the whipping-horse, her petticoats (which had not been removed) over her head and her back parts bare, while her hands were fixed fast in the rings; forgetting the significative humiliating pose of my dear mother, Betsy ran to the house of the nearest doctor, who did not happen to be Baker's usual medical attendant.

Entering the corridor, the first object that met his eye was my mother. He first set her free, then turned to Baker whom he found to have been dead for twenty minutes.

What can I add?

My mother has no thought of another and third marriage, young, beautiful, and charming though she is. We live together and she

---

[2]   All orders for books and applications for catalogues to be made to « Edition Parisienne, » 66, Boulevard Magenta, Paris-X^e.

finds my loving companionship sufficient.

As for me doubtless I shall some day meet the girl whom I shall wish to make the adornment of my hearth. She will love and honour my dear mother, who in turn, will give her good counsel and love her as a daughter.

If it be God's will I shall have children.

But neither boys nor girls of mine shall ever know the oppression of the corset. Their boots shall be of the comfortable, practical, flat-heeled English type.

Glazed kid in any shape or colour shall be ever "taboo" in my house.

I hope that no little boy of mine will ever be dressed as a girl and called by a girl's name. And I express the same hope in regard to all other little boys.

For had not my darling mother delivered me in time I should have lost for ever my honour and my manhood.

THE END.

TABLE OF CHAPTERS

BIRCHGROVE PRESS
Flagellant & Libertine Erotica

———————

Birchgrove Press specializes in producing new print and e-book editions of pre-1950s writings on sexual flagellation in English. Original editions of many of the books that we offer are difficult to obtain and are highly sought after. We are especially proud to offer new editions of rare Victorian flagellant texts such as *The Mysteries of Verbena House*, *Experimental Lecture by Colonel Spanker*, and *The Quintessence of Birch Discipline*. Birchgrove Press also produces new editions of libertine literature. We have published *Venus in the Cloister*, *The School of Venus*, *The Dialogues of Luisa Sigea*, and Isidore Liseux's translation of the Marquis de Sade's *Justine* (1791), *Opus Sadicum*, for example. For a full list of titles and formats, please visit our website:

www.birchgrovepress.com.

www.ingramcontent.com/pod-product-compliance
Lightning Source LLC
Chambersburg PA
CBHW072000170626
46813CB00005B/1944